Crumbs from the Edge

A Collection of Short Stories

Char Bishop

These stories are works of fiction, products
of the author's imagination. Any resemblance to
actual names, persons, events, or places is coincidental.

Published by
Char Bishop
P. O. Box 5392
Sun City West AZ 85376-5392

ISBN 097004660X
ISBN 978-0-9700466-0-4

Dedication

This book is dedicated to my daughter Christa Federico, for "buttering the edges" with her unconditional encouragement and support.

And to John Federico
who made certain my stories were as polished
as they could be by providing gently honest
critiques, often right-on editing suggestions, and meticulous
proofreading

CONTENTS

Introduction

"Butter the edges of the toast and the middle will take care of itself," an old saying that seems to have faded away with time, was told to me by a 93-year-old friend. His grammar school teacher drummed it into his students' heads but left its interpretation up to their imaginations.

In this collection of short stories, "Buttering the edges" means taking everything into account before you act, laying the groundwork, paying attention to details, so everything comes together in an orderly manner.

"Crumbs from the Edge" are stories about some people who buttered the edges, and others who didn't and got stuck in the middle.

Iguazu

Only seven members of the large Worlds Unlimited travel group elected to make the side trip from Rio in a refurbished military plane to the local airstrip near the border of Argentina and Brazil to view the Iguazu Falls.

From the air strip, they traveled by van through the jungle to the river upstream of the falls. A single woman getting over a contested divorce had a silver flask that kept her misery in check. A newlywed couple sat behind her.

The driver guided the van on a slalom course around the washed-out pockets of the road. The blond wife braced herself on the arm rest and hissed at her husband that this was not the honeymoon she'd had in mind. The husband ignored her and glowered at two strikingly handsome young men who held hands beneath a cardigan stretched across their laps while they shared a laugh with their handsome foreheads nearly touching.

Across from them an older couple in expensive resort attire appeared pre-occupied with their thoughts, oblivious to the lush natural beauty of the tropical terrain. The man was not well. He said he'd stupidly drunk water from the lavatory sink at the airstrip to take aspirin. The office manager had given him a bottle of fruit juice, but instead of improving, he had begun to vomit. The van made a number of stops. He apologized profusely to everyone. The driver said he'd probably picked up a parasite.

On the way to the falls, they passed a jeep parked at the side of the road. A photographer was loading camera cases and a tripod into the back of the vehicle. He gave them a brief wave as they passed. The husband and wife locked eyes. He sighed and leaned back, seeming to relax.

A mile farther up the road, the van parked on a dirt strip next to the river, where two large wooden row boats were tied to the shore at the edge of the powerful flow of the mile-and-a-half-wide Iguazu River. A couple of hundred yards downstream the river fanned out into 272 separate falls that fell nearly 300 feet to the river below.

Before the *turistas* had a chance to rethink their decisions to take what was a thrilling but risky sightseeing trip, they were hustled into the two boats, each manned by a brawny mestizo rower. As the rowers labored across the heavy flow of the river, their perspiring naked chests rippled with the strain.

The two handsome men laughed with nervous excitement as the boat side-slipped in the current. The blond bride had her hands over her eyes until they arrived at a rocky, shrub-covered island near the lip of the falls where the rowers slid the two canoes up onto the rocks far enough to secure them to the shrubs against the tug of the water, and helped the passengers out.

The group walked out on a rickety wet boardwalk to view the thundering cascades. Only the older couple stood together a distance away, where the husband vomited repeatedly over the rail, his wife patting his back.

He eventually spoke in halting Portuguese to the first rower who agreed for a *gorjeta*, a tip, to row him back to the shore ahead of the other passengers so he could rest in the van. The man's wife gave him a light kiss and said she would stay, that she wanted to enjoy the marvel of the falls.

The first canoe did not return for its passengers. The remaining rower waited a long time. Ultimately the group had little choice but to split into two groups. The rower would take the first group to shore and then would return for the second group. The wife of the sick man was eager to see how her husband was faring back on land, and was allowed in the first group.

When they arrived back at the shore, they found the van driver attending to the limp and barely coherent first rower who was lying on the sandy bank. He interpreted the rower's recounting of his boat overturning and the rower jumping out and being swept close enough to the shoreline so that he was able to swim to safety.

The driver reported to the wife that the boat had then gone over the falls with the husband clinging to it. She slipped to the ground in a faint. The driver and the honeymooning husband carried her to the van.

When the van returned the group to the sightseeing service's office, the manager contacted the authorities. The wife, wringing her hands, demanded they send a search party at once to look along the river below, that her husband was a strong swimmer and might still be alive.

The office personnel exchanged dubious glances. Because of the height of the falls and the power of the water, they said, they could not offer her hope that either her husband or the boat would be found. Nevertheless they assured her a search party would be dispatched.

She broke down and cried then. After she'd composed herself, she handed the office manager a business card and told him her husband was expected to return to New York for an important meeting in two days. She wasn't calm enough to call his company to inform them of the accident, and would the manager be so kind as to do so.

On the return flight to Rio, she sat apart from the group, wordlessly staring out the window from behind her large dark sunglasses. As her fellow travelers exited the plane at Galeão International Airport, nearly each one paused to extend condolences

3

or a few feeble words of encouragement that her husband would be found.

Back at her hotel in Ipanema Beach she unpacked her bag and threw an empty bottle of Ipecac into the waste basket.

He didn't call her that evening. Their plan was that he would take a private charter flight back to Rio, then pick up a fake passport in Rio before continuing on to Andorra. Their plans were for her to return to the States and have a memorial service for him, then take the time she needed to wrap up all their business matters. She would join him at Christmas.

Her husband didn't deserve to go to prison. After all the years he'd cooked the books for his damned company, keeping it from going under, what little he'd transferred out of the country for them wasn't sufficient payback. Now he suspected the officers, who had been paying themselves huge salaries and bonuses, while he worked for a pittance, were planning to pin everything on him. Despite her conservative upbringing, she didn't feel a morsel of guilt over what they were doing. The company owed them.

Even the sightseeing company didn't hold out much hope that they'd find his body, so how could the company ever prove he wasn't dead?

He'd told her she should relax and indulge herself while waiting for his call. After all, they could afford it. So she did: visits to the resort spa, new clothes, dancing with gigolos in the hotel bar in the evenings, and treating herself to the Colombian emerald ring she'd always wanted.

Three days later he still hadn't called. By this time her stomach was in an anxious knot and she experienced qualms that she'd never had in their twenty-eight year marriage. Was he really in Andorra? Or had he used her for this ploy to fake his death, obtain falsified papers, and buy enough time so he could disappear? Perhaps the account was in the Virgin

Islands or Turks and Caicos instead. Making the contacts, setting up the account, planning their strategy had all been taken care of by her husband. She was no longer reassured by the fact that it was a numbered account and he had given her the number as a safety measure. She had relied on him completely for everything.

Finally she called the hotel in Andorra where they were to meet. No, he hadn't checked in, but he'd made a deposit for a two-week stay, so they hadn't cancelled his reservation. How stupid did he think she was? The cost of two weeks even at such a luxurious hotel to throw her off track was negligible compared to what he'd funneled into their account. Their account? Was it, really? Now she wasn't so sure.

That night she went dancing at the hotel bar. A movie star-handsome man sitting at the bar next to her bought her a second martini. She was sure she hadn't had too much to drink but he'd somehow ended up in her room. The next morning she awoke on top of the bed covers, still dressed in her evening dress, her underwear unruffled, her makeup and hair still perfect, but her emerald ring was missing.

In her modest one-piece swimsuit, with its slimming skirt to flatter her ample hips and derriere, she went sunbathing on Ipanema Beach. The abundance of tanned Latin beauties strolling around in string bikinis that exposed their oiled, firm buttocks made her sick. With the money that he'd diverted to his account, he could afford to have one of these sluts lying next to him on the beach on whatever island he ended up at.

She considered going to Andorra, visiting the bank and verifying that the account was actually there, but she had no fake papers and passport yet. Her travel would be traceable.

When she returned from sunbathing, the hotel clerk told her she'd gotten a call but the gentleman refused to leave a message. He would call back at 4:00.

5

Finally! Worry lifted from her like a nightmare dissipating on awakening.

At 4:00 exactly her in-room telephone rang and she snatched it up. "Where have you been?"

"*Desculpe,* Senhora*?*"

"Oh—who is this?"

"It is Senhor Basurto of the Worlds Unlimited Travel. I'm most distressed to tell you, Madam, that your husband's body has been recovered."

She could barely take in her next breath. "What?"

The man stammered with discomfort as he repeated his announcement.

"No! No!" she shouted. "He can't be dead."

"*Sim,* Senhora. We found his passport in a black money belt that he was wearing. It is him, I am most regretful to tell you. If you can give us the name and telephone number of your lawyer, then we can make arrangements to send him back to the United States." He spoke of details, of shipping *the deceased*. She was stunned beyond comprehending any of it.

What had gone wrong? She would call the travel office at Iguazu and ask to talk to the rower. No, of course, that would be stupid. He was not going to admit that he'd had an agreement with her husband to fake his drowning—especially now when he could be charged with accessory to murder. Besides, she remembered he spoke no English.

Ah, the photographer! No. He'd looked too savvy to admit he was waiting for the rower and her husband to get out of the boat near where he was parked in his jeep, before they let the empty boat go over the falls.

She assured Senhor Basurto that she would have her lawyer get in touch with him and hung up.

The room was deadly quiet. It wasn't the same room anymore. She wasn't the same angry, suspicious—and mistaken—woman. If she could have him back again she would give up every wretched penny in that damned account. But it wasn't possible. Of course he hadn't tried to cheat her. All the while she'd been waiting for his call she'd indulged herself, then misjudged him and accused him while he lay dead on some river bank in the jungle.

As soon as she could compose herself she called their lawyer in New York. She was too shocked to comprehend what he was telling her, only that she was not to worry, that he'd make the transportation arrangements. That done, she asked the concierge to book the next flight available to New York. Then she packed. She had to be home when her beloved husband's remains arrived.

She decided she would go ahead with their plan. There would be a memorial service, then she would conclude all their outstanding business matters and sell their home. She would be in Andorra by Christmas.

When she was informed by her lawyer that her husband's body had arrived in New York, she went to the Regency Funeral Home. She was seated in a salon with his closed casket and given a package containing whatever personal effects were on him when he was found.

After the mortician left her, she opened the torn and bruised money belt. There were various receipts, nearly washed clean of any ink. His water-damaged US passport was there, the stamps inside unreadable ink blotches. She didn't know where he had planned to pick up his fake documents before flying on to Andorra. There was so much he didn't discuss with her. She'd always relied on him.

In the belt was a small billfold containing U.S. credit cards, some Brazilian *reals* and U.S. dollars. She felt a stab of loss when she saw the puckered plastic sleeve containing two snapshots, back to back, of the two of them in Hawaii. They were taken many years ago, happy times long before he got involved in trying to keep his company from going under.

When she pulled the molding, sticky photos from the sleeve to see them more clearly, a bank debit card sandwiched between them fell into her lap. She immediately guessed it must be the ATM card for the Andorra bank that he said he had.

At least there was one bright note to his body being found. The card would make it easier for her to access the account in Andorra.

Then she read the card and her bottomless grief erupted into molten fury.

It was for a bank she'd never heard of, a bank in the Grand Cayman Islands.

Down at Club Stinkaroo

"You'll get your throat cut one of these nights, hanging around places like that," said my friend Dora, as we sat across from each other enjoying an espresso. "It seems there would be a safer, more respectable way to learn to play Texas Hold'Em to impress your sisters when they come into town for your family reunion."

I'd felt the same way when I first started playing. "The bars that host these free Texas Hold'Em tournaments to get new customers are careful to see that the games are run orderly," I explained. I thought I'd better not bring up the late night tournaments, scheduled for the working class who came into some of the sports bars to drink, for off-track betting, or a game of pool. By *working class* I meant stable hands from the racetrack, garbage truck drivers, and construction laborers.

Some were unemployed and disempowered by the depressed economy. It was a place where they could enjoy a few minutes of glory for winning at pool, for coming in first at a free poker tournament or for cashing a winning ticket at the off-track betting window for Mom's Fat Dancer in the 4th at the local track.

Dora screwed up her face as though she'd just taken a bite of a spoiled apple. "Who hangs around those places so late? Probably gang boys celebrating a street fight victory, or scum who've just forklifted an ATM from the local bank drive-through and need a little 80 proof refreshment."

"They're okay. They just live a different lifestyle," I said, remembering I'd felt the same when I first started playing the free Hold'Em tournaments. Dora, too, might benefit from some exposure to the way others lived. She might have gotten a taste of reality by playing with Marcus at the Blue Olive Bar who told me he'd just gotten out on parole, or been as mesmerized as I had been when I first saw some of the regulars at Mick's Down Under Lounge, whose bodies were totally laced with tattoos —from what I could see, anyway.

Dora didn't look convinced, so I said, "Even the folks from Sunset Ridge Village flock over to the Monday afternoon game at Mario's Vesuvius Restaurant," I explained. "They enjoy a poker lunch special and a social afternoon. The ladies show off their grandkids' photos and the men vie for each other's stack of chips."

I didn't add that even with a portable oxygen machine or a walker the men could still engage in competition, *mano a mano*, so to speak. As tempted as I was—just to make my point —I wasn't going to snitch on Pastor Meeker's sister who played at the restaurant regularly, all dolled up. The men certainly had their eyes on her large stacks.

The night I went to my first tournament at Club Stinkaroo, I nearly gagged on air thick with stale booze smell. Clouds of cigarette smoke wafting in from those hanging around outside mingled with work-day body odors

My family would have lost control of their natural functions if they saw me, the only woman sitting at cards with eight men, tattooed, unshaven, a few in hoodies hiding behind dark glasses, whose table conversation was lavishly spiced with the "F-ing" word.

Dora continued scolding in her prim, clipped tone, "What would your sisters think, a dignified woman like you playing with lowlifes like that?"

I smiled, thinking about her reaction if she could have seen me at a high round bar table, the sausage-like arms of the corpulent twin Edam brothers pushing in on me from either side, me clutching my cards above our kissing elbows, while any time a rap number came

10

blaring from the jukebox, a Jamaican man would jump up and dance, his dreadlocks whipping about his face.

As for my sisters, I didn't think they would question where I was playing cards as much as *why*. I was the black sheep in a family of insatiable card players. As I was growing up, Mom and Dad's social life consisted mainly of Saturday night card games. Adults crowded around the dining room table for poker while my three sisters and I sat at card tables with cousins, playing Old Maid and Go Fish.

When we became teenagers we were allowed to join the grown-ups' table but it was far too serious for me. I yearned to be back at the kids' table, engaging in silly fun, caring not a fig who won or lost. I wasn't at ease with the adults' taunting, gloating, or engaging in arms-in-the-air self-celebratory shouting. I couldn't understand the heated family arguments if winning pots were divvied up incorrectly a few cents one way or the other.

Right after I got married, Jerry, my husband, played cards with us, but before long he chose to park himself in front of the TV in another room watching the history channel, happy to be out of the fray.

Over the years my sisters and their families relocated to other states, but in July of each year at the family reunion the Saturday card game marathon was the featured event, sometimes lasting until 3:00 or 4:00 in the morning. I thought it best to let my mother know this year there would be a conflict.

"That Saturday is the Annual Southwest Found Art Show. I have pieces entered in the show and I'm going to be there." I expected some resistance, but I was not going to back down on this. I'd spent weeks in smelly bars with some less than desirable dudes to learn to play in order to join in the game with my family; I expected a bit of reciprocal courtesy when I asked them to spend an hour to share my first exhibit of my "found art."

"But we're all together just once a year," Mom argued, "and we *always* play on Saturday night."

She finally suggested we might take a short break at 5:00 p.m. so the whole family could go to my show, and then resume the game at 6:00. Given that my sisters had never shown the mildest bit of interest in my art work, I could picture the lack of enthusiasm with which they'd receive *that* news.

Since the previous family gathering my sisters had caught on to the craze of Texas Hold'Em poker. I'd heard about the free tournaments being held around town and thought maybe I could learn before the reunion so I wouldn't once again embarrass myself by being the grand loser. I read two beginners' books from the library. Then I dressed in Levis and an old sweatshirt—which I guessed might be the appropriate garb—and set out for the trenches.

When I walked into the Club Stinkaroo I hesitated just inside the door so my eyes could adjust to the darkness of the windowless bar. It was one long narrow room, big enough to squeeze in two pool tables and four tall round bar tables with stools. The bar itself ran down one side, ending at the back where an off-track betting window was located. Three televisions mounted above the bar tables televising live sporting events from around the world competed with rap music blaring from the jukebox and the cap pistol cracks of pool cues.

The game manager seemed to recognize me as a newcomer to the free tournament and waved me over. "Sign up here," he said, handing me a clipboard with a player log-in sheet.

I sat down at my assigned table with six men and one woman, Mable, who gave me a warm smile, exposing a mouth only half full of teeth before her face melted back into its comatose poker expression. I shuffled the cards sloppily, an obvious clue that I was a novice. My allotted chips disappeared faster than the

12

complimentary chili hot dogs set out on one end of the bar.

A big man called Lumberjack, who'd actually worked as an axe man in the forests of the Northern California coast, dealt me the final blow with his full house beating my three cards of a king. "Sorry, Girlie," he said.

I read a few more poker books before my next tournament at Mario's. The clientele were a different bunch altogether, retirees from the nearby senior community. They had played poker for nearly a lifetime, and they played a tight, smart game. I watched and learned. I caught on to observing "tells," subtle mannerisms that were clues to whether a player was bluffing.

These old guys were good, and hard to "read." Mr. Eardley, a frail, tiny man who'd recently lost his wife, found the tournaments a distraction from his loneliness. He had a great poker face but when he was dealt a good hand, his excitement caused his ears to redden and everyone fold their cards.

Contestants who were eliminated as the game moved along were sent off with polite farewells, an occasional "Good game!" or a friendly apology for having been ousted from the game. These players didn't gloat when they won, or whine or throw their chips across the table when they lost. At Mario's I learned how to play a *gentleman's game.*

Sukkup's Bar was another matter. The young men there were dressed in hoodies and spoke street lingo. They had an *in-your-face* style that could turn a newbie like me into a bowl of quivering jelly as they easily maneuvered me into betting all my chips on a questionable hand.

A young hothead named Digger played loose and bluffed all the time. He also made clear his opinion that poker was a man's game. When he won he would snarl, "Yes, yes! Come to Papa!" making a grand and gloating show of using both arms to sweep his chips toward him. His behavior reminded me of my family's style of gamesmanship and made me all the more determined to learn to play a *gentleman's game.*

When I was reassured that Andy, the game supervisor, kept a lid on tempers and discouraged locker-room language and risqué jokes, I calmed down enough to concentrate on my play.

I carefully studied Digger's style. I only had a pair of deuces but I suspected he was bluffing when he raised. I reraised, and so it went, back and forth, until we both had all our chips in the pot. It was pure luck that a third deuce came up on the flop and I was able to knock him out of the game with three cards of a kind.

I was nervous because I didn't know how he would accept taking a licking from a woman. He shoved his stool back from the table, glowered at me from beneath his billed cap and grunted. "Good hand, Mom." After that I was called Mom by all the young men there, which I didn't find particularly complimentary, but Max, a highway construction flagman, assured me it was a mark of respect.

I learned what I should've learned from playing with my competitive family: there are no friends in Hold'Em. You take no prisoners—you give no quarter. Anything you hear is white noise, either players letting off steam, trying to convince you they are beginners so you'll let down your guard, or trying to confuse you into incorrectly guessing their hands.

Lumberjack asked me, "Why you so fixed on learning to play this game? You don't seem like yer enjoying it that much."

I told him I was the black sheep of my card-loving family and I was tired of having a target on my back. The next time I went to the club he set a little plastic figure of a donkey in front of me.

"That, Girlie, is a 'donkey.' In poker it's a person who doesn't care enough about the game to learn to play right, and is the player who everyone makes a jackass out of. That's going to stay in front of you until you get the idea."

Each time Lumberjack won a pot from me, he explained why he won and why I lost. He taught me the post-oak bluff and the semi-bluff. He explained how the belly buster straight and the double belly buster straight worked. I read more books from the library.

One night I felt I was finally understanding the game when three suited cards were turned up on the flop and Lumberjack's face was so empty of expression it gave him away. I guessed he probably had two cards of the same suit in his hand and held a five-card flush. But there were still two cards to be dealt, either of which could give me a full house that would beat him, which was what happened.

"Guess you spanked my ass," he said, grinning. He put the plastic donkey in his pocket and I never saw it again.

At break time I went to sit next to him at the bar and bought him a beer to thank him for coaching me.

"You know," he said, "some fellers just don't seem to win much at life. So now and again they win at poker, and they can show 'em— show 'em that they're not a loser, show 'em that they're good enough, show 'em that they're man enough.

"But remember, no one wins all the time—in poker or in life. Sometimes you're gonna lose, not because you're a bad player; it's just someone else's turn. No matter how good you get, the cards will decide who's gonna win. How good you play the cards you're dealt with, having a little fun, playing nice, losing with grace, that's what makes a real winner."

With those golden words of social gamesmanship, I was ready when my family arrived for the reunion and we sat down for the legendary Saturday night poker game.

"Let's play a couple rounds to teach Marla," my

15

sister Pattie suggested.

"I've been playing with friends," I said. "I think I know the basics."

Pattie rolled her eyes comically at everyone and they all chuckled. "Okaaay, if you say so." She shuffled snappily and dealt, the cards sailing just high enough to land precisely in front of each player.

For the first hour I knew I was playing right, but I got trash cards. I started to feel like I always did when I played with the family: like a loser. We were an hour or so into the game, and after the customary triumphant whooping and table thumping on the part of the winners, everyone had taken a portion of my chips leaving me nearly bankrupt.

Then *it* happened: the who-gets-the-good-cards needle of Lady Luck's compass swung around the table, and stopped, pointing squarely at me. I got unbeatable cards, and play after play I won back my losings. My heartbeat galloped with elation. After years of being steamrolled by my sisters, I wanted to pound the table and scream, "Yes! Yes! Take that!" But I played nice, just as Lumberjack taught me.

At 5:00 o'clock Jerry emerged from his safe zone in front of the living room TV and said we ought to get over to the gallery. Chaos erupted. Accusations of "poor sport" and "take-the-money-and-run" rained down on me. When I got up from my chair, Pattie put her hands on my shoulders and pushed me back down into my chair.

"Just another half hour," she insisted. A half hour later I had nearly everyone's chips. This donkey was not going to get her ass kicked this time.

After the negotiated half hour passed, Jerry's effort to break up the game so we could all get over to the gallery met with unanimous grousing.

"Come *on*, Marla," my sister Marylou whined, "you know we *always* play cards on Saturday night."

"Just come to the gallery for an hour, then we'll

16

come back and take up where we left off," I coaxed. My answer was a table full of pained expressions.

I looked down at the mountain of chips in front of me. "If this is so important, I'll save you all some trouble." I divided the chips into equal stacks, and shoved a stack to each player. An embarrassed silence swept over the table.

As Jerry and I wordlessly gathered our things to leave, no one made a move to join us. I guessed they were about as interested in going to see a bunch of soldered-together old junk as I was in finishing the card game. Before we were even out the front door, I heard the snap of Marylou shuffling the cards for the next round.

At the gallery things were lively. Jerry stood across the room, grinning proudly at me over a glass of passably good merlot. Visitors clustered around me, listening with genuine interest as I explained how I'd constructed my largest "found art piece," an indoor waterfall made from old car parts.

We stayed until the exhibit closed, after which we relaxed on a bench in the gallery garden polishing off the last bottle of champagne. I was warmed by a glow that went deeper than the mellowness brought on by the wine. That night, not just I, but everyone at the exhibit, had been a winner: the genuine art lovers who regularly attended shows; those who, for lack of anything better to do, came for complimentary wine and refreshments and to mingle, the customers who bought my pieces, and the gallery owner who was happily affixing red "sold" dots next to a number of my pieces.

This was my kind of game. Okay, I admit I did mentally whoop and yell "Yes, yes!" as I observed people enjoying my artwork, and more of them than I could have hoped for actually buying.

I haven't been back to Club Stinkaroo, nor have I played poker since. I'd learned that the most lasting satisfaction comes from choosing your own game, not one that others choose for you, what you give to that game, what you take away, and a win-win outcome for all the players.

Powder Burns

Was it 3:40 or 8:20? The pumped howling of
coyotes on the hunt on the Pebblestone Golf Course
sounded like a bunch of shrieking children surrounding
a birthday piñata. Their cries always left him cold. The
good thing was that one more damned rabbit was not
going to ravage Alice's pathetic flower bed. He wondered
what made women think they could have a flower bed
that could survive triple-digit summer days in the
Arizona desert anyway.

There was no sunrise halo around the edges of
the bedroom's closed vertical blinds yet. A choir of
bullfrogs on the golf course pond belched out a pre-dawn
serenade, sounding like a bunch of constipated cows.

He blinked a few times, squinted, and then
reached for his glasses next to the clock on the bed
stand. *3:40 a.m. Damn.* Waking up this early was just a
fluke. For 72 years he'd been healthy enough to get a
good eight hours of sleep each night, not like his
neighbors, whose lights went on around 2:00 a.m. or
3:00 a.m. They couldn't sleep, they complained. It's just
a part of growing old, Frank offered condescendingly,
mentally assuring himself that it was them growing old
and not him.

People often commented that Frank had the
energy of someone twenty years younger. He didn't
whine and complain about every little ache and pain
instead of paying attention to the game. People who

didn't take golf seriously should stay the hell off the course.

Getting out of bed, he concentrated on keeping his balance on the way to the kitchen. His arthritis was the worst on rising, but, hey, a half hour of loosening up and he was good to go.

Alice was still asleep, snoring. She didn't perform the stentorian arias she accused him of the nights she fled their room for the quiet of the guest room. He was not caving in to her suggestion of separate bedrooms just yet. That was the last thing he was going to give up. Age robbed you, one by one, of the things you once took for granted, but things you just didn't have the energy for anymore. He still had potency to make love to Alice. That would be the last thing he'd give up.

In the kitchen he poured himself a large glass of orange juice. The sugar boost always fueled him up for his morning walk around the course. He opened the back door. The temperature was a little cooler on this overcast August monsoon night. The darkness was thick with a heavy wet silence that newcomers to the retirement community often found a bit creepy. It was too early for the quail to greet the dawn with their coded calls to each other. The coyotes were quiet now, probably back from their night hunt and sleeping in their dens beneath the huge thicket at the center of the course.

Frank's walking buddies, Gerry and Ralph, wouldn't be up yet. In a couple hours the three men would meet for their daily cardio walk around the course before it opened for play. Aw, heck, he thought, restless for something to do to make the time pass. Why wait for the old buggers? He was up and ready to go, too awake to get back to sleep again. He'd go on ahead, and when he didn't show up to meet them at the street corner, they'd probably figure he was taking Alice to an early doc's appointment.

He returned to the bedroom and changed out of

his pajamas. Alice's light snoring stopped abruptly.

"Frank, what in God's name *are* you doing?" she mumbled. "It's the middle of the night."

"I'm up, so I might as well get my walk over with."

"Is that a good idea? I mean it's so...dark out there since the Golf Commission voted to turn out all the course lights after midnight."

"I'll take the new LED flashlight."

"The sprinklers go on at night. And those coyotes—we had too many pups this spring. Four of them attacked Jane Baker's terrier early the other morning—Stu came out with his Big Bertha club and beat them off, but Jane had to take the dog to the emergency pet clinic."

"I'm not a 10-pound dog, Alice, for chrissakes. You women are such worry warts. Besides, I called the Game & Fish Department last week and I'm sure they culled the pack by now."

"Oh, did you have to do *that?*" she wailed, suddenly coming fully awake and sitting up.

"They just relocate them out to the desert," he said irritably,

"They don't, Frank. That's something they tell the residents so they don't feel bad. They *euthanize* them," she retorted.

"Whatever works," he answered.

Alice let out an exasperated sigh, which she seemed to do often these days, and lay down again, pulling the covers over her.

Nag, nag, nag, he thought, as he took an appraising look at his naked body in the mirror. His gut seemed bigger. He sucked in his stomach, puffing out his chest, which momentarily gave him the appearance of being more buff than he was. Too bad he couldn't keep it that way.

The good thing was everything important still worked, and with no kudos to erectile dysfunction medication. He felt a flush of macho pride as he looked at his reflection in the mirror. How many of his buddies could look like this and still perform the way he did?

On second thought, maybe he didn't want to go for a walk. He went over to the bed and sat down, running his hand back and forth over the generous swell of Alice's hip beneath the blankets, their permission signal. Her arm, heavy with sleep, swatted his hand away. The signal turned yellow.

"Stop it, Frank. You know I don't like it when I'm half asleep." She rolled over, turning her back to him. Red light.

He shrugged. So what else was new? He slipped into some sweatpants and his favorite cotton gecko print shirt. It was practically falling apart from endless washings, but he'd had it so long it had become his signature shirt. "Gecko Man!" he thought, flexing his biceps.

As he went through the kitchen on his way out the back door, he felt a little hungry. He could take a snack to eat when he stopped to rest at the ninth tee. He rummaged through the bread cabinet and took out a large French roll and slid it in one pocket. In the fridge he found slices of ham leftover from last night's dinner, which he slipped into a fold-over sandwich bag and then wrapped a couple leaves of Romaine lettuce in a paper towel, shoving both into the other pocket.

He'd be able to finish the loop around the course long before the temperature started rising, around 6:00 a.m. or so. Gerry and Ralph would probably only be half way around by that time. Frank would be home enjoying sausage patties, Alice's potato pancakes with fresh bacon pieces, fried eggs and a cup of rich dark French Roast, while the guys were discussing the virtues of slow-cooked steel-cut oatmeal with flaxseed.

Out on the driveway he paused for a moment. The street felt closed in by thick, wet darkness. He'd never gone out this early. Usually it was light by the time the guys were on the trail. Realizing he'd forgotten the flashlight, he decided not to bother.

He chuckled at the visual of Gerry rattling his soda can filled with pebbles at the occasional coyote that loped across the golf cart trail. One coyote didn't bother Frank, but they ran in packs on the course. He went back into his garage and got his 7 iron. It had worked on the big male swan that had threatened his golf foursome last week near the pond by the second hole.

It was over before the group could say anything. They stood looking at the big swan, lying in a nest of its bloody feathers. They thought he'd overreacted, saying that one ticked-off swan wasn't much of a match for four golfers. They hadn't invited him to join them since. Frank was sure they were afraid they were going to get involved in his hassle with the Golf Ccommission over the killing of the swan. As Frank saw it, the swan wasn't paying golf course dues and fees; he was.

His footsteps echoed loudly on the sidewalk. The only street light was at the intersection a half block away. It filtered through the heavy umbrella of trees, falling in a peppered pattern on the sidewalk. This late into the night the solar lights bordering driveways had dimmed to almost nothing. Frank felt a frisson of caution. Maybe it was too early, after all, to start out. He looked around, expecting a couple coyotes to lope into view. Or maybe a javelina. Hadn't seen one of those for months, but they were around.

Desert Palms Senior Retirement community lay on the fringe of a Phoenix suburb, surrounded by wide open desert. Who knew what was stalking around out there at night? Wild animals came into the community when driven by the need for water or food.

Some of the wives insisted they'd seen a bobcat running through the green belt behind their houses. Probably just female hysterics. Still, he thought it would be kind of neat to see one of those bobcats catch a rabbit. He wondered, could they bring down a coyote?

Or one of the javelinas? He imagined those little tusked bastards could be pretty fierce if they were cornered.

He remembered the first time he'd seen javelinas. They were all sizes, seven of them, walking single file, crossing the road to a drainage canal that opened out onto the desert. An old boar took the position of sweep at the end of the string.

They were there at man's good graces, thought Frank. What was it the Bible said, "Conquer the animals of the land and sea"? He had tromped on the accelerator then and had himself a good laugh when the old boar bucked out of the way, limping arthritically across the course to catch up to the herd. He envisioned the animal's hoary head mounted on the wall of his study.

Frank reached the intersection of Golf Course Drive where the circle of the streetlight cast deep shadows on the bushes along the sides of homes adjacent to the street. A slight rustling in a nearby bush caused him to veer off the walk, an automatic response in snake country. In the summer they occasionally were out at night.

When he reached the clubhouse the sky was still inky black. Frank got a firmer grip on his 7 iron and started out around the front nine. The houses surrounding the course were vague silhouettes against the distant street lights, with a few pinpoints of light showing here and there through windows. As he walked, the sound of his muted footsteps on the trail was magnified by the intense quiet. Fading solar lights on patios cast light on the trail for no more than twenty or so feet ahead.

As Frank picked up his pace he could feel his pulse throbbing in his ears. He suddenly heard howling on the far side of the course and felt a spike of adrenaline prickle his arms. Coyotes. A sudden halt to the noise indicated they'd probably brought down their prey. They were busy. He didn't have to worry.

24

He moved on at a faster pace. As he approached the pond near the second hole, he was aware of the absence of the bullfrogs' bawling. Their night chorus meant everything was safe and secure until its unending refrain ceased. Why was it so quiet, he wondered? He started thinking this early walk was a stupid idea. No one to bullshit with. It was going to be a long walk without Gerry and Ralph's yammering.

The pond was nearby, but not visible in the starless night. He was unprepared for the sudden stab of tightness in his chest. Walking too fast, he guessed, and stopped to bend over and take a few deep breaths.

Just then he was able to make out Stan Patterson's house with the nymph statues surrounding the backyard pool dimly lit by a couple of dim solar landscape lights. Suddenly the trail before him blurred into a charcoal wall. He lurched forward, trying to stay upright, but his outstretched hands were grasping at nothing but air. His vision returned, and to one side a white blur appeared. He squinted and was able to make out a large swan and two cygnets coming from the direction of the pond.

He pitched forward and his hands shot out to break his fall. The 7 iron flew to one side. He slammed onto the asphalt trail and rolled onto his back. He could feel the racing of his heartbeat in every pulse point in his body. What the hell was happening? He looked up at the inky flat sky that seemed just inches above his face, and then mentally laughed at his clumsiness for a nanosecond. He'd never fallen on the trail before. Must've been a crack in the damned asphalt.

His body felt like it weighed a thousand pounds. His back seemed fused to the pavement. The swan and her cygnets were closing in on him now, white sail-less ships bobbing in a sea of night. From where he lay they appeared to balloon to immense size as they approached, chattering in clipped conspiratorial squawks.

25

They moved closer, making him nervous. He commanded his body to move, but felt nothing. When the female came at him in a rush, his eyes closed defensively. He felt the incredible strength of her huge wings as she flapped furiously onto on his supine body.

When she looked down at his face, the Pattersons' landscape lights revealed an odd questioning in her yellow eyes. The young swans crowded up behind her, nervously swaying from foot to foot.

Her gaze hardened into determination, startling him. He suddenly remembered the male swan he'd killed by the pond. His hands reached around him, feeling for the 7 iron, but it was gone.

A shout of alarm escaped him when he felt the stabbing peck of her beak on his stomach, pulling at his shirt. The morning air was suddenly cold on his naked skin. The cygnets leapt up behind her, and followed her example, tearing at his shirt and pecking at his body. A button flew off and hit him in the forehead. A feather caught in his eye. Night turned into a flurry of feathered wings.

"Get off," he mouthed the words, but fear squeezed his throat and shut off the sound. With superhuman effort born of panic, he hoisted himself upwards, spilling the attacking swans off him.

They scrambled out of the way as he dragged his leaden body to his feet. He managed to get upright. His eyes, barely focusing, made out the golf cart path a few feet away. He stumbled back to it. The 7 iron was not in sight.

The swans fled. His arms and legs felt as though they were made of rubber. All he could think of was getting home. Out of the fog of his confusion, desperation helped him recall the private alleyway between the houses that was a shortcut back to his own street. The path sharpened into focus. Relief washed over him as his disorientation eased. He'd find that alleyway and get himself home for a good bracing cup of coffee. He was sure getting up too early made him feel this way.

As he blundered along the trail, he sensed, rather than heard, something keeping pace in the blackness behind him. He had to focus what little energy he could muster on finding the alleyway; there was none left to pay attention to the small squat figures trotting alongside him. They stunk. Javelinas.

One moment he saw the path ahead; the next, gravity spun him around and his own weight and bulk spilled him onto the trail. He lay on his stomach weighed down by confusion between a starless sky above and hard wet ground below.

Sounds of snorting and snuffling surrounded him. Wet muzzles nudged curiously at his still body. He wondered in a spurt of panic if javelinas were carnivorous. He could feel the boar's tusks and long hard snout pressing beneath his arm, like a front loader.

The boar poked and shoved at his side, the tusks tugging at the already torn shirt. All at once Frank felt the pressure of the javelina jabbing his side. In a fit of unthinking panic, he edged away, managing to turn onto his back. The smell of the animal was foul. The other javelinas circled around Frank, nudging and prodding at his body, gasping with loud excited breaths.

He became aware of a sticky wetness on his shirt front and sides. His looked down at the slope of his belly. There were dark splotches on his shirt. Blood. But he was so numb with panic he felt nothing. God, was he going to have to spend his last moments on earth watching some wild pigs tear him apart?

He felt hot tears of outrage fill his eyes. Summoning whatever strength he might have left, he willed his arm to move. To his relief, it rose, feeling like a fifty-pound lead weight, but flailing feebly at the boar. The javelinas, startled by Frank's sudden arousal, squealed in panic and scurried away, filling the night

27

with their chattering chorus of alarm. He pressed his fists into his stomach, hoping it would contain the bleeding.

Frenzied with fear, Frank's adrenaline rush helped him get up on his hands and knees. His head ached so badly he thought it would split in two.

His equilibrium cleared, allowing him to get one foot planted on the ground and to struggle up to a standing position. His hand went involuntarily to the oozing on his shirt front. It was heavy and thick. The javelinas must have gored him. The swans probably cut him with their beaks.

Spurred on by hope regained he staggered along the pathway, searching in the darkness for the familiar alleyway. It had to be close by, but he couldn't see a break in the dark row of homes along the course.

As he continued on, his adrenaline eased and he felt a profound weariness. His pace slowed. He had to get off the damned course to a side street where folks taking early morning walks with their mutts could help him.

With a jolt of useless hindsight, he realized that if Gerry and Ralph were with him…well, he had to get back on his own. Hadn't he always? He didn't need Gerry or Ralph, damn them. This was all *their* fault, always oversleeping, having to walk later and later in the morning, with their this-ache and that-ache. Damn them, he wasn't walking with them anymore.

A soft rosy ribbon of light appeared close to the horizon. Unaccountably, Frank felt tears sting his eyes at the sight of it. With dawn breaking he would find the alleyway.

Before he could finish the thought, everything dissolved into a gray blur as he pitched forward to one side, falling into the dewy grass. His face was pressed into the earth, and even with all the effort he summoned, he could not move. His lips, parched dry from fear, were soothed by the feel of the wet grass, but he gagged at the chemical taint of pesticide. It was a familiar smell, the same chemical he spread on his lawn, the same crap that Alice insisted killed the newborn wild rabbits. He was down for the count and knew it. He felt nothing but an increasing heaviness press on his body.

In a delusional stab of humor, he thought about the headlines in the local throwaway newspaper: "Frank Carter pecked and gored to death by swans and javelinas on the golf course."

His eyes fluttered closed and he drifted. Alice, oddly, crossed his thoughts. He envisioned her in the kitchen, grating potatoes for the pancakes, nagging him about how his cholesterol was going to give him a stroke and he would die young, as his parents did.

At one point he thought he saw movement nearby, but realizing he had no fight left in him, he closed his eyes and surrendered to his weariness. A whimpering sound brought his eyes open again. A dog! Finally, someone walking their dog on the golf cart path. He'd complained about that a lot, but there were still the idiots who let their dogs poop all over the golf cart path.

Hope escaped him like a deflating balloon. The brightening dawn showed the unmistakable outline of a pack of circling coyotes. The big alpha male was a few feet from him, head hung low, appraising, intimidating yellow-green eyes leveled at him.

The animals edged closer. Rough noses nudged at his body, searching, prodding, smelling, Shying away at his slightest move, then returning to explore. The air was thick with the smell of wet pelt. Something gnawed at his shoelace and he felt his shoe tugged from his foot. The animals closed in on him, nuzzling him. He felt the full weight of one of the critters standing on his back.

He made an attempt to shout, which came out as pitiful mewling. Then he tried again, contracting his stomach. His agonized groan startled the coyotes, and they ducked and swung away from him. Frank knew he had to get up. They'd probably smelled the blood oozing from where the swans got at him. He could handle one coyote-- or even two, if...he thought of the 7 Iron left far behind.

His head felt as if it would explode from the mental effort of commanding his body to move. Then he felt hot tears of futility tracking down the sides of his cheeks. His shame at them, and his anger at possibly having his life end in such a humiliating way, roused him enough to clamber up on all fours. He began to move heavily, edging along like a wounded buffalo.

The animals were tailing him, curiously approaching him when he paused, and then slinking away when he moved. In the murky distance rose a long low silhouette. *Please, let it be the groundskeepers' mowing equipment.* The increasing daylight didn't help him get his bearings. He was off the trail and everything around him was reeling.

When his head lifted, his heart plummeted. It wasn't the groundskeeper's cart and wagon ahead. With gut-wrenching clarity he made out directly in front of him the impenetrable thicket golfers called Coyote Island. It was his last horrified thought as he fell to the ground and felt the full weight of the coyote pack upon him, snapping and growling at each other to lunge at his exposed chest and stomach. There was no sight or sound beyond that, just the foul smell of coyote saliva on his face and the certainty that he was a goner before he blacked out.

The wet pelt smell of the coyotes drifted, became lighter, evolved into a faint antiseptic odor. The oxygen from a cannula in his nose cleared his head enough for him to see Alice sitting next to his hospital bed, reading a paperback. He closed his eyes and surrendered to immense relief and the blissful fog of exhaustion and drugs.

While Frank was in the hospital bed hooked up

to monitors, his attempts to understand the multiple attacks on his golf course walk were interspersed with nightmares of swans, javelinas and coyotes dragging him into the thickets and devouring him. He was struggling with just such a medicated dream when Alice gently shook him awake.

"Frank, it's all right. You're safe," she soothed.

Spurred by desperation to escape the nightmare, he managed to struggle through the haze of medication to wakefulness.

"Swansh aschtak me." *What was wrong with his voice?* His mouth felt like it was stuffed with a handful of Alice's cosmetic cotton balls.

"Gerry and Ralph found you, Frank, lying off the cart path. The doctor said you had a series of strokes."

"Shlavaleena omme," he whispered urgently. When he reached across the hospital bed to grasp her arm, Alice removed his hand and patted it. "It'll be all right," she said. "The doctor says you should recover your speech just fine with physical therapy."

Whenever Frank attempted to tell Alice about the attacks in garbled two- or three-word phrases, she shushed him. "It's the medication, Frank. Try not to talk. You're safe now and you need to rest and heal." Gerry and Ralph also had doctor's orders not to agitate Frank by letting him talk about the incident.

After hospitalization and rehab, Frank began to regain his ability to speak. One morning the fall weather was balmy enough for Alice to serve their breakfast on the open patio: steel cut oats and fresh fruit and decaf coffee.

When three coyotes loped along the green belt behind their home, Frank let out a startled yell and fumbled for his cane with a shaking hand that didn't work so well yet. Alice looked up from her paperback book. "It's okay. Since I planted my herb garden and you haven't been able to use that horrid pesticide, there are more rabbits, so the coyotes are hanging around."

31

The critters hesitated, eyeing Frank, and then trotted away.

One evening, Alice and Frank were enjoying the single daily glass of wine that the doctor now allowed him, when a javelina boar came through the open space behind their home. He trotted within a few feet of the patio, stopping briefly to snuffle longingly around Alice's small herb garden encased in a cocoon of protective chicken wire. Frank froze with fear, speechless and trembling until after the javelina had moved on.

Another time, the mother swan and her cygnets came waddling through the green belt while Frank and Alice were having breakfast on the patio. Stronger now, Frank took up his cane, intending to fend them off, but Alice gripped his wrist. Her look was not sympathetic.

"Frank, that morning, when Gerry and Ralph took their walk at the usual time, they found small tufts of bread on the pathway. You know how Gerry is; he gets so upset when someone feeds the swans because it brings them away from the safety of the pond to where the coyotes can get them. Then they found your 7 iron near the cart path at a spot where the grass was all dug up. The groundskeeper said there were javelina prints and some bits of lettuce on the ground.

"Further along the trail the guys saw some black liquid on the path—"

"Yes, yes," Frank interrupted, agitated by the memory, "the blood from the tusks."

"There wasn't much blood. Just a few beak pecks on your chest and stomach that they bandaged up at the hospital after they wiped away the motor oil from landscaper's mower spill on the cart path. Gerry and Ralph figured you must have slipped and fallen in it, because when they found you by the coyote island, you had it all over your shirt."

"You mean when the coyotes were attacking me—"

"No. On the green where a pup was chewing up

one of your running shoes."

"That's when the coyotes were attacking me and tearing off my clothes," Frank insisted, his voice escalating at the memory of his terror.

"Ralph said the coyotes were wrestling over a plastic sandwich bag with ham in it." Alice had told him eating so much ham would be the death of him. He just didn't think that was what she meant.

"Anyway, Gerry shooed them away with his coke can."

Frank imagined Gerry, who was terrified of coyotes, courageously holding his ground, shaking his soda can full of pebbles at the pack. But he didn't like the barely concealed amusement in Alice's voice.

"The last two pieces were missing from the refrigerator drawer so I figured it was yours." Frank felt a flush of reality wash over him. He was silent for a very long time, as he began to make sense of his distorted impressions of that night.

The next week when Alice and Frank were having their morning coffee on the patio, the female swan came with the adolescents. She paraded her children very near to the patio.

Frank felt immense relief when he saw a large male swan following close behind them chattering and diverting the female and the young ones away from the house.

"I thought they mated for life," he said and felt some of the guilt he didn't realize he held inside him ease.

"Not always. Just like people, there are times when a new mate is necessary," she said. They watched the foursome waddle away down the greenbelt.

"Something you should keep in mind," she added pointedly, and went back to reading her paperback and leaving him with a number of things he needed to think about.

Final Sentence

Mariah had never seen the ghostly, chalky blue marks on the old trees, or the blue plastic ribbons knotted around their trunks, blowing with such deceptive gaiety in the afternoon coastal breeze. She had come to the Northern California coast from San Francisco, a city girl unfamiliar with the raw beauty of the Northern coastline and the rape of the old growth forests by the lumber industry.

She'd decided to make a lone trip high and deep into the Northern California coastal mountains to an old growth forest. The enormity of the primeval forest, with trees hundreds of years old and hundreds of feet high, overwhelmed her.

The ancient forest was witness to how insignificant and brief her own time on earth was in comparison. The spiritual ambiance of the grove infused every pore of her body and was absorbed into her bloodstream. It was disorienting, as though she had been hypnotized into some ritualistic trance. However, it had the opposite effect of thoughtless abandon fueled by spiritual fervor; instead she was overcome with an immense peace, a certainty that Something, Someone with the power and wisdom to create such a miracle was moving us around on the chessboard of eternity with love and purpose.

She walked alone through the blessed silence of the forest, broken only by birdsong and the wind whispering in the parasols of branches far above her. Neighbors had explained a blue chalk mark or blue plastic streamer signified the tree was marked for felling. It would be downed, dismembered, its bark stripped, and its bleeding, raw trunk dragged to the mill to be fed into the maws of the mill blades. What took dozens of generations to grow would be gone in weeks. The giants that stood up to time and the vagaries of nature, that gave home and sustenance to the animals of the forests, would not have the chance to succumb to age and the forces of nature to lie on the forest floor and devote their decaying bodies to nurse seedlings that would replace them and sustain the forests naturally.

Mariah visited those woods many times. It was akin to visiting inmates on death row. She would linger at each tree bearing the condemning blue swath of paint. The ribbon brought to mind a funereal armband. Sadness for its loss weighed heavily on her, like a last visit to a dying friend.

One day she chanced on a tree located a distance from others. It was magnificent and grand. Because it stood apart and was not sheltered by the shade of other trees, its trunk was able to absorb the heat of the mid-afternoon sun. She held her arms up to embrace it, able to encircle only a meager portion of its immense diameter.

She lay her cheek against the bark and pressed her encircling arms and body against the trunk. The heat of the day became the life heat of a fellow living organism of the earth. The soul of the tree seemed to communicate with her own.

Mariah thought upon Chief Seattle's wise words in 1854:

"Humankind has not woven the web of life. We are but one thread within it. Whatever we do to the web, we do to ourselves. All things are bound together. All things connect."

She understood the message of the environmentalists who chained themselves to trees, driven by their desperation because not enough people understood or cared about the disappearing giants, abducted with nothing left to sustain the forests.

Work took her back to the city. When it seemed

that life weighed too heavily on her she would return to walk among the trees. She would smell them and touch them, always coming away with a sense of wonder at their strength and endurance, always diminished by them, but also inspired and comforted by their existence, which gave truth and tribute to their Maker.

Some of the trees she'd walked amongst on previous visits were gone. All that was left were savaged stumps. The open space left by their theft was an ugliness that went beyond ripped, sap-oozing roots and rendered limbs that no longer provided homes for endangered animals; it was a spiritual vacuum, made all the more poignant by the life still standing around it. Standing and waiting. For what? A similar fate? Or waiting for man to realize that he was undermining his own existence.

Dancing on the Other Side

Maggie entered the lobby and through the double doors she could see the Parkland Ballroom was full of milling guests. Across the room the orchestra was tuning up.

It was all she could do to keep herself from leaving before anyone saw her. It wasn't that she had no courage. She'd resuscitated four people who'd suffered heart attacks, been nearly choked to death by an agitated Alzheimer's patient, and carried a woman fifty pounds heavier than herself to her car to rush her to the hospital before her massive stroke did its damage.

But tonight she felt every bit as apprehensive as the first time she had attended the Parkland Boomers Mixer, the first and only time she had. The memory of it still had the power to make her stomach twist. Perhaps after tonight it wouldn't.

In the gold baroque mirror over a marble side table in the entryway she saw a beautiful woman. It still felt as if she were looking through a window at someone else, a stranger with a shimmering upsweep of platinum hair, expertly applied makeup, and no double chin or plus size hips.

Even months after her surgeries, she was still confused by her reflection in a mirror or storefront window. She had to remind herself she wasn't *good old Maggie* anymore. Now she, Margaret, could walk into that room, could hold her head up, and unequivocally belong.

But the old unworthy Maggie tried to pull her back, coaxing her to flee to the safety of a place where the women didn't patronize her and the men didn't look through her. Instead, she took another glance in the mirror and smiled. Dazzling veneers shone from a perfectly colored mouth. She inhaled deeply. She was ready.

In the ballroom the guests who came as couples were seated at tables of four on one side of the broad dance floor. On the other side were the ladies and gentlemen of the Parkland Singles Club. A lot of boomers were moving into the senior community. The singles' side had considerably more seating ringed in a half moon facing the dance floor than when she'd last come three years previous.

The Saturday night Boomers Mixers had drawn a good crowd. Maggie spotted an empty chair and headed for it, dodging the waitpersons delivering trays of lubricating cocktails.

Just as she was about to sit on an unoccupied chair, a sequined evening bag was slapped down on the seat. "Sorry, this is taken." Maggie recognized the speaker, one of a clique of a dozen women who were the founding members of the singles group. The woman locked eyes with her, her tight smile not quite rising to the level of apology. Maggie saw the woman didn't recognize her.

Down the line at the very edge of the semi-circle she saw another vacant seat and headed for it. An arm came down over the chair like a crossing gate, sans red lights and bells.

"Taken!" The woman looked anorexic, her skin drawn over the harsh angles of her face like a latex glove over a bony hand. Maggie remembered her and her little charade of claiming the chair next to her was taken with the hope that one of the male guests would sit by her during the evening.

Maggie located the head waitperson at the bar directing his staff. He accepted the large bill she pressed discreetly into his hand and swept a chair from a vacant table at the back of the room, hefting it across the dance floor with Maggie following.

The moving of chairs was forbidden, and unprecedented. The manager had overseen the dances for two decades, and when he told the guests at the center of the semicircle to rise and nudge their chairs a few inches either way, there were a few raised eyebrows, some grumbling, but no outright disobedience. She let her eyes sweep down the line with a wide smile, nodding her thanks. The returned looks were a combination of irritation, appraisal, curiosity, and, most satisfying, unconcealed interest on the part of the men.

No sooner had she sat down and settled her jet evening bag in her lap than a young waitress came over to her.

"The guy in the red jacket would like to buy you a drink." The girl nodded in the direction of a tall, too thin, bald man. He was an elder in her church. The few times she was able to get away from her former duties to attend services he'd always seated her at the rear of the church. She gave the girl her order for a double martini. It was going to be an interesting evening.

His mouth was permanently drawn in a disapproving curve, except when he smiled, which he did when Maggie nodded her thanks at him and let her gaze drop demurely to her lap.

She was all too aware that some people would see her as a cliché', the senior class fatty who shows up at the high school reunion after shedding 100 pounds and thumbs her nose at the football hero who spurned her, or the female nerd, turned down by the sorority she pledged, who returns to her alma mater to parade her successful rise to CEO of her multi-national company.

Not one iota of shame was going to spoil the satisfaction she would enjoy tonight, indulging her fantasy, delivering to certain guests their comeuppance. No sooner had the band begun to play than dancers were filling the floor. Two men approached Maggie and asked her to dance, neither of them willing to give in to the other. Maggie held out her hand to the least attractive, most socially awkward of the two and let him lead her onto the floor. He was a poor dancer, but she had learned at Davina's Dance Academy on the far side of the city, to lead and yet let your partner feel he was leading.

There were two fellows who she was certain would not ask her to dance. Dancing was not what she had in mind. She swayed over to the first man, who sat next to his date, and boldly asked him to dance. His date, Carol, whom Maggie knew well, obviously didn't recognize her. The woman put a possessive hand on her escort's forearm. Maggie flashed a smile at her and pulled him to his feet, knowing that he would be too embarrassed to refuse.

"We're old friends. I'll just keep him for one dance, I promise," she said, and felt his reluctance and embarrassment as she firmly grasped his hands. It had all happened so quickly, Carol sat open-mouthed as the couple walked onto the dance floor together.

"I used to live here, you remember?" Maggie said. Turning his back to his fuming lady, he took Maggie into his arms.

"That's not possible. I would recognize you, my dear,"

"I was caretaker for Carol's mother before she passed," Maggie told him, waiting for the revelation to sink in, which came pretty fast.

"You're—Maggie?"

"Mother liked to call me that. I'm Margaret now. Not Maggie anymore."

"No, you certainly aren't," he said. He didn't attempt to converse further. When the music stopped, he thanked her and fled back to Carol, shaking his head. When he sat, he immediately leaned over to her to give her the news, Margaret was certain. The woman was a gossip, and Maggie knew that word of who she was would spread rapidly around the room. She had a few more things to accomplish before it did.

She looked around the circle of chairs. There was a tall gentleman, and she was certain she'd known him from somewhere, but couldn't remember. He was casually dressed, in a way that suited his relaxed manner. His eyes were on her, bright with interest. At one point he caught Maggie's eye and gave her a wide smile, which she found easy to return.

But her intent tonight was to announce her return to Parkland, in the most rewarding manner. She would never again be Maggie, the invisible drudge. She stood and glided across the floor to the ladies room. In the bathroom mirror she saw that she was holding up fine. She also saw behind her a very familiar face, and she turned.

"Dottie!"

The plain, rather poorly dressed woman's expression turned from guarded to openly pleased. "I knew it was you, Maggie." Dottie had worked as a postal clerk for many years and knew everyone.

"Where did you go? And...and..."

Maggie bent down and looked beneath the stall doors to make sure there was no one eavesdropping. Then she took the woman's hand and they sat down in the small adjoining lounge.

"This is just between us, Dot. You remember I moved in with mother after Harold died. It worked for both of us because I had a place to live and she didn't have to go to residential care. And you know we had other women boarding with us?"

"I know, Maggie. Some of those ladies must have been difficult to care for. I heard Melina Moore had Alzheimer's, and Betty Dutton had a stroke and was in a wheelchair. Bless your heart. It must have been hard for you all those years."

"They were nice ladies, but when Mom passed I was glad to let the bank foreclose on the reverse mortgage. I couldn't afford it. I got an adequate little apartment and took a clerical position at the Lark Residential Care Facility. I was still *good old Maggie*. I hungered to have more than that in my life, but when Harold was alive he'd lost most of our savings investing in the stock market, so all I was left with was Mother's small savings account."

"I'm so sorry to hear that," Dottie said. Then she raised her eyebrows as her gaze swept over Maggie's stunning gown and the dazzling rings on her fingers.

"One day I got a telephone call from my father's attorney. He and my mother had divorced when I was a toddler, so it was a shock. He'd been married to someone else all his life and had no children. His wife passed away and then he died shortly after.

"His trust specified that if there were no heirs all would go to charity. Thank goodness the trust lawyer found me. I was heartbroken that my father never cared to make contact, but his lawyer told me his wife forbade it. I guess in a moment of remorse my father had him draw up the trust so it wouldn't have my name in it, but specified by its terms that I would get his estate by virtue of being the only heir.

"Finally I could afford to—shall we say—get a little tune-up. I was so tired of people looking down their noses at *good old Maggie*. I'm Margaret now."

"I'm glad that your life is easier. Working at the post office I got to know most people in this community. Some of them are a real pain-in-the-you-know-what. The people whose opinion I value liked you. They appreciated you for taking care of your mother—and many of their mothers and sisters."

Maggie sighed. "Thanks, Dot. What I've done to myself isn't about vanity as much as it is about just wanting people to accept me. Do you understand what I mean? If I do move back I hope we'll continue to be friends."

"Gosh, I think I'm outta your league now." Dottie grinned.

Maggie let out a very unladylike snort. "Oh, pooh to that."

"All this," she said patting her hair, and wiggling her be-ringed fingers, "is just to show everyone I'm just as good as they are. Underneath it I'm still Maggie."

A guest entered the ladies' room, and the two women rose to leave.

"I've always liked *good old Maggie*," Dot whispered.

By agreement Maggie walked back to the ballroom by herself so she could continue with her charade.

The woman who'd blocked her from a vacant chair when she'd first arrived was Bea Reeds. She had been the president of the singles group for many years, and was nicknamed the Queen Bea. Maggie had taken care of her sister for six years and she'd had to endure Bea's patronizing manner during that time.

Marty, Bea's partner, was the only man who'd asked Maggie to dance the one time she'd come to the Boomers Mixers. Jealous, Bea circulated some ugly remarks about Maggie that night.

Now Maggie saw that Marty stifled a yawn behind a closed fist, only half listening to Bea's chatter. She caught his eye, and smiled at him. He stared at her for a moment, his brows drawn together in concentration.

Then he sent her a cautious half smile in return. It was all she needed. She rose and approached him, her head high and her smile beaming around the room on her way, as though the dance was in her honor.

"Bea, you don't mind if Marty dances just this one little dance with me, do you?"

Maggie's nerve startled Bea momentarily. The struggle to decide if she knew Maggie was evident in her skewed expression.

"Well, not if he really wants to—it's *certainly* up to him."

"Of course, he does. If I remember, he was a pretty good dancer." Maggie held out her hand to him and he looked helplessly from one woman to the other, like a mouse trapped between two hungry cats.

Without looking at Bea, he mumbled, "Excuse me," in her direction and rose to put his hand lightly on Maggie's back to lead her onto the floor.

"Please forgive me," he said. "I think we've met. I just can't place where."

"Yes, we have. Here, at a Boomers Mixer, but it's been three years. I don't expect you to remember, but I do. I was seated right there in the middle where Bea is sitting and you were the only man who asked me to dance."

"I couldn't have been the only man who asked—" He looked her over with frank appreciation.

"Let's say I'm not the same woman, Marty. I wasn't well when I left and I've healed up, with the help of a lot of good doctors. I'm Maggie Davenport." She didn't elaborate that most of the doctors were plastic surgeons and two were psychologists.

Marty stopped dancing, his mouth slightly agape. "Not Maggie—"

"Yes, *good old Maggie*. I'm feeling so much better now."

"I can't believe it." he murmured, picking up the dance step again to cover his fluster.

"Don't you think the doctors took good care of me?" she smiled at him and winked.

"I most certainly do. You look so healthy and—energetic."

And not fat, she knew he was thinking. *No wattle. No rippling buttocks.*

The music came to an end.

"Well, welcome back, Maggie," Marty said.

"It's Margaret now. I'm sure we'll be running into each. Don't forget."

He led her back to her chair, and returned to Bea

who waited with a frosty expression and her arms folded across her chest.

Maggie was searching through her bag for a Kleenex when an open, inviting hand appeared before her. She looked up, and thought, "Oh, this is going to be perfect."

Mike LeGrande had lost none of his flash and sparkle. He wore a white dinner jacket and black tie and looked ready for a world cruise and dinner at the Captain's table. He was the person she'd hoped most to see.

"May I have this dance, lovely lady?"

She looked up at the patrician face, shaved to within a hairbreadth of skinning, blue eyes that had paled but still held a sparkle, and too-white teeth. The tan was probably real as Mike was an avid golfer. She couldn't help it; that old queasy, unsettled feeling when he looked at her was still there.

How she'd longed for him to see her the one other time she'd been to the dance. He had sat down next to her much of that night, and other than a brief nod had not bothered to even talk to her. She had seen him often around their smallish retirement community, and he'd always looked right through her, not even bothering to say a polite hello at the supermarket, or in line at the bank. Now his eyes were flicking over her with obvious relish.

The orchestra was playing a tango. She stood and let him sweep her out onto the floor. He pulled her into some basic steps, to test her, she was sure, so she added some flamboyant moves that her dance instructor had drilled into her, giving him the clue that she was up to whatever he could dish out. His eyebrows shot up in exaggerated surprise. He eagerly spun her into the next step, dipping her backwards.

The dancers around them fell back like a receding tide to watch them execute advanced moves with grace and precision, embellished with quite a few

47

faux sultry looks. When it was over they received enthusiastic applause and Mike lead her to a quiet corner table. His face was flushed with excitement.

"Why do I feel we've met, yet I don't think we have because I know I wouldn't have forgotten you," he said, after ordering champagne from the circulating waitperson.

"I've lived here before, but moved away a few years back."

"And you're back—thank goodness," he said smoothly, patting her hand.

"Yes. Well, I remember *you*, Mike. We didn't know each other but I would have liked that."

"I can't believe we wouldn't have gotten together." He meant *date*. He'd dated so many women in the community that those many women who turned away his frisky demands had formed an in-name only group known as the "Less than LeGrande Society."

"Oh, yes. Believe it, Mike."

The champagne came, a whole bottle in a bucket in an elaborate stand. It was an expensive Grand Cru.

Mike saw that she was studying the label.

"Mike LeGrand only orders Grand Cru for grand ladies," he said. She wondered how many hundreds of times he'd used that line.

They sipped their champagne and his eyes swept over her, his gaze containing the barest suggestion of a leer. She encouraged him, looking out from beneath lowered lids that promised a whole lot more than she had any intention of delivering.

Instead of asking about where they'd met before, showing any interest in who she was, he launched right into a drawn-out description of himself and his life.

He finished his drink faster than she did, and his free hand moved closer to her, until it fell below the table and lightly brushed hers which lay on her thigh. His fingers toyed with the huge diamond ring on her hand. She saw by his interest in it that he had no idea it

48

was nothing more than a beautifully crafted flashy CZ, cubic zirconium.

After some light banter he looked into her eyes. "Now, tell me, why wouldn't I have known you? Why wouldn't we have met? Didn't you come to the dances then?"

"I did—once. You sat down next to me four different times and never so much as said 'hello' to me." Remembering that, she could no longer maintain her forced smile.

"Not possible!"

"You looked right through me," she said, nodding, her tone regretful.

"Couldn't happen. You are too stunning a woman."

"Let's just say I'm not who I used to be. My name was Maggie Davenport."

"Maggie?" he murmured. He frowned in concentration as he locked his gaze on her sapphire earrings. "I didn't know a Maggie—Oh, not the caregiver who took care of the bridge ladies' mothers!"

She flashed a smile at him as if he'd just guessed the first round on the Millionaire game show. "That's the one! So you did know who I was, then?"

"Of course, my lady friends spoke of you, and what a blessing it was to have you help them with their daughterly duties."

"I'm sure."

"My dear, you offered a wonderful service," he said, his tone a little too insistent.

Service, she thought. *That was it, she was 'in service,' a drudge, an hourly employee. Someone you didn't acknowledge socially. Certainly someone you didn't lower yourself to dance with.*

Maggie persisted, getting closer to skewering him. "It's odd that when I saw you around town, you didn't seem to know who I was."

"Well, you know, er—we didn't have a working

relationship," he said lamely.

"Hmm, I see. Well, we won't have a working relationship now either."

"Most surely not. He picked up her hand and moved it a bit so the light could catch the facets of the diamond. "You've apparently come into some beneficial circumstance, Maggie."

"Money, Mike, lots of money. Money can work miracles. And you can call me Margaret—Maggie's gone. Poof, no more."

"The name certainly suits you."

"Yes, it does."

"Enough chit-chat," he said, pouring them each another glass of champagne. "Let's drink a toast to us, Margaret. You are enchanting. Will you have dinner with me?"

"Oh, I think not," she said in an unnecessarily loud voice, her tone dripping with boredom.

His expression turned to stone. Bright rosy spots appeared in his cheeks. "Have I done something to offend you?"

"We don't run in the same circles, didn't before— and surely won't now." She set the champagne glass down firmly.

"This is rather bad champagne, Mike. Not what I'm used to. I hope you're not insulted if I don't finish mine."

She stood. He seemed frozen into place by her rebuff.

Maggie turned her back on him and walked away, feeling suddenly deflated. She'd thought it would be fun to give all these snoots their comeuppance, liberating her from past hurts. All it had done was dredge up a lot of painful memories. Memories that didn't seem to matter any longer.

Did she really care enough about any of them to be concerned about their opinion of her? She didn't like any of them. She didn't care for Margaret much either.

She crossed the dance floor on her way to the cloak room, when she saw the tall handsome gentleman who'd been watching her stand and hurry to intercept her.

"Pardon me, but I was hoping to ask you for a dance," he said. The first thing she noticed about him was the gentleness in his eyes. He had a receding hairline and beautiful silver hair. His generic sports jacket was a soft dove gray under which he wore a polo shirt. He did not seem like he belonged in this crowd.

As attracted as she was to him, Maggie had had enough of the Parkland Singles.

"I'm sorry, but I was just leaving."

"If you're leaving, then there's no reason for me to stay. May I walk you out to your car?"

She smiled at the subtle compliment and they went to get her coat.

"Would you mind holding this for a moment?"

He took the coat and she walked back into the ballroom past the half circle of guests. A few of them saw her and whispered to each other. She found Dottie sitting at the far end of the line with two women who clerked at Bartlett's Market.

She bent over and hugged her. "Goodnight, Dot. I'll see you very soon."

"Goodnight, Margaret."

As she walked back to the lobby she nodded, smiled, and waved at everyone on her way out of the room. "Goodbye. Goodbye," she sang. It definitely was goodbye, not just goodnight.

She and the stranger crossed the parking lot, taking their time.

"I'm Dick Carnes."

"Margaret Cummings."

"I know who you are," he said, smiling. "Do you mind?"

"Why would I mind?"

"Because it seems you've reinvented yourself,

and I didn't know if you wanted me to blow your cover."

Maggie stared hard at him for a moment. Her first thought was that he was making fun of her. Then she saw he was sincere. She started to chuckle, and before she knew it, she was laughing until tears ran down her cheeks. She laughed until she was completely drained of her bitterness.

She pulled a Kleenex from her purse and dabbed at her eyes. "Oh, my cover is so blown already, not to worry. I do recognize you, but I can't recall from where."

"And I'd be willing to bet you've had others say that to you all evening long."

"Okay, I give up. How do you know me?"

"My Aunt Lorena had a stroke and couldn't be alone in her own home. She boarded at your mother's home for many months. I lived on the east coast then and was only able to visit her a few times a year.

"When I came here on business I would pick her up and take her out for the day so I never had much of a chance to say more than 'hello' to you.

"I remember you because she wrote me often and never failed to talk about your kindness to her and the other ladies. She even sent photos of you with the other guests. I almost felt I knew you."

Maggie's brows shot up in surprise then. She did remember Lorena Carnes and the many caring letters from her favorite nephew.

"Yes, now I do remember."

For the first time that evening, Margaret felt her heart smile.

He held out his hand for her car key and opened the door for her. She felt his other hand beneath her elbow steadying her as she got in. It was a delicious feeling, being the one coddled for a change.

"My aunt willed her home to me and I'm living in Parkland now. I hope you'll give me a chance to know you better, Margaret."

Maggie remembered, then, when he'd come to

pick up her aunt to take her out for the day, how happily Lorena had clung to his arm. She imagined herself clinging to his arm and said, "Yes, I'd like that, Dick.

"And, by the way, to you it's still Maggie. Just Maggie."

She took the business card he gave her and drove away, her heart still smiling.

A Few Grains of Sand

He was small and brown and his baggy swim trunks hung loose around his stick thin legs. He terrorized the seagulls with his delighted shouts and arms windmilling with joy. The tall man who stood soberly to one side watching him was pale, blond, with scant body hair and a sullen expression. His posture resembled a wet shirt on a laundry line.

On the dark sand at the surf line, the boy's mother played keep-away with his small sister. The woman was thin and dark like the boy, wearing a loose white cotton blouse and a long gauzy gypsy skirt, which the afternoon wind pressed against the angular outlines of her body. As she ran after the girl, her fine, long raven hair whipped about, a bleeding ink smudge against the cerulean sky.

The boy chased a gull directly in front of his mother, then halted and clapped his hands so that it rose and fluttered out of her path. Pleased with himself, he clasped her about the waist and cried, "I saved you, Mom." She froze a moment, then peeled his arms from about her and bolted towards the water, where his sister was shuffling curiously towards the hungry waves.

Watching the explosion of life on the San Diego beach fascinated me. The air was heavy with the scent of coconut suntan oil and grilling hot dogs. It was not at all like my home on the remote northern coast of the California, where the beach that I naively considered "my beach" smelled like a pungent soup from the sea, salty with the living and fly-dotted with the decaying.

I had moved there in the summer when the remote shoreline lay flat and glistening with untrammeled sand and natural flotsam—not the discarded potato chip bags, forgotten beach towels and torn flip flops that pepper a southern bathing beach.

In the summer my beach opened the endless reaches of its isolated arms to receive golden sand gifted to the shore by the gentle sea in contoured patterns, sometimes as fluted as a pie crust, other times like sinuous snakes braided with tumbled sea grasses and tiny twinkling shells. Over the summer months, a few grains of sand at a time, the coastline swelled into a wide golden ribbon.

It was no longer my beach when winter came and the coastline was assaulted by storms. The ocean retched tangles of uprooted seaweed, an agonized tree trunk ripped from the forested coastline further north, an occasional dead otter, or a gasping fish stranded by the ebbing tide that I could still throw back into the waves. It gnawed away at the coastline until it reclaimed all that it had given during the summer. Summer and winter, the flood and ebb of the sea reflected life itself, giving, then taking away again, a few grains of sand at a time.

My attention was drawn back to the curious little group in the sand between me and the shore. Neither the man nor the woman had wedding bands. He the blond white Nordic God; she the sultry gypsy queen. It was easy to guess that their physical differences attracted them to each other.

The children were dark and intense, and appeared to possess the unbridled nature of their mother. He was bland and arrogant, his attitude one of having only to exist in the world in order to justify his place in it. In any case, it seemed so, as he stood aside and let the slight boy struggle alone to skewer the pole of a beach umbrella into the sand.

The child had not planted the pole sufficiently

deep in the sand to hold fast in the strong breeze. The man glanced at the wavering pole, but turned away, stretching languidly. Minutes later the umbrella took a full gulp of wind and toppled. The woman turned and told the boy to try again, then looked up at the sun and shielded her eyes with her hand.

The boy had learned something by his fruitless labor. This time he took up his sister's sand shovel to excavate a very deep hole. His twiggy arms aimed the tottering pole into the hole, thrust and twisted, his tender mouth screwed up with effort. The man watched the child struggling with his task for a few moments, yawned with disinterest, then went to the woman standing at the edge of the shore to run his hand possessively over her back as they shared the sight of the sparkling surf.

The umbrella was upright in the sand, but it wobbled as small gusts threatened to topple it. The boy sat back on his heels a minute, appraising his work, then proceeded to pack handfuls of sand high around the base of the pole. Satisfied that it was secure, he rose and went to his mother and pointed to the umbrella. Distracted by her companion nuzzling her neck, she merely nodded not bothering to look. The boy stumbled away from the couple, his shoulders hunched.

The couple touched each other in suggestive ways, as if the beach weren't crowded with onlookers. The little girl reclaimed her shovel and knelt in the hard sand with her back to the water, her toes licked by sea foam.

The boy had returned to his mother's side. He rocked from one foot to the other and tugged insistently at his mother's hand to gain her attention. Without warning, the man scooped him up and ran down with him to the surf, flinging him into the chilly waves. He strolled back up to the woman. His hearty laugh had a ring to it that had nothing to do with amusement.

Spindly dark arms rose out of the water flailing

57

in the rough surf, until the boy finally got his footing in the shallow water. His expression was dark as he stomped up to the couple and circled around the man to pound his small fists against his fleshy, pale back.

The man again swept up his puny attacker, rolled him in the sand, over and over, until he resembled a heavily sugared donut. He returned to the woman, folded his arms across his chest, and rocked back on his heels, smirking.

The boy struggled to his feet, mouth open in a soundless "O" of outrage. Swiping the sand from his eyes with his forearm, he plodded back to the blanket beneath the umbrella and wrapped an oversized striped beach towel about himself. The brightly covered folds around his head didn't hide his murderous expression.

His mother glanced around her and noticed him missing. She turned and waved to him to join her, but he stayed next to the umbrella. After two unsuccessful attempts to summon him, she went to him and entreated him to make a sand castle with his sister, but his feet were placed wide apart in the sand and his clutched the towel as tightly as if it were armor against further bullying by the man.

Eventually the mother returned to the blanket, sitting on the windward side of the pole to lie beneath the shade it offered. She lifted her cloak of hair to expose her neck to the cooling breeze. The man lay down on the opposite side of the pole, stretched out like overfed cat getting settled on a warm window sill, and closed his eyes.

The rising afternoon wind buffeted the umbrella pole but it held fast. The victor dozed on the downwind side of the pole and the fair maiden he'd won sunned herself on the other side. The boy lay between them on his stomach, his forehead resting on folded arms.

Moments later his hand unfolded from beneath his head and inched slowly toward the pole, like a small lizard, pumping with caution a few seconds, and then sliding a few inches farther. He absent-mindedly started brushing away a handful of sand here and there from the base of the pole.

I watched as the wind and the small excavating hand worked in concert to loosen the umbrella's purchase in the sand. I doubted the boy realized the possible outcome of his action, that a flying umbrella caught up by such a strong wind could become lethal weapon. I considered whether I should stop the inevitable, yet I couldn't interfere. The scene would be played out. Just as the ocean changed the character of my beach a few grains at a time, so would this child be changed by his small life choices.

After a few minutes of furtive digging, the pole began to rock in the wind. A brisk gust picked it up, like a giant hand yanking it from the sand. It came down on the sleeping man. The overturned umbrella blocked my view of what was happening, but I heard his cursing and the distressed cry of the woman.

The boy jumped up and stumbled to one side, surprised at the success of his mission. Then he turned towards the ocean and folded his arms. He set his feet apart, puffed out his flat stomach and looked at the sea through narrowed eyes.

The woman rolled the umbrella to one side and I saw that the man's flaccid midsection was smeared with blood where the end of the umbrella had raked him. She knelt over him as he clutched at his stomach, and took a tissue from her bag to wipe away the smear and inspect the wound. After she dabbed the small gash, it immediately welled up with blood again.

"Alonzo," she called, "get the first aid kit from the car."

The boy turned and dragged his feet in long slow steps across the short distance between them to take the keys from her hand.

"Go, go," she urged. He loped off, weaving amongst the beach blankets, running lazy circles around groups of sunbathers. The woman took a few more tissues and pressed them onto the man's stomach. When he moaned dramatically, she turned away and her eyes rolled upwards.

In the parking lot the boy was walking heel to toe on the white painted lines of the empty parking slots. It was awhile before he returned to hand his mother the kit. "Here, Mom. I hurried."

She looked unsmilingly into the boy's eyes. "I know."

He watched as his mother gently cleaned the wound and covered it with a number of insufficiently small band aids. Tears welled up in his eyes and he turned and ran down to the ocean, running full on into the frigid waves. The man continued to lie in the sun with his eyes closed, gingerly touching his bandaged wound.

The woman and her daughter gathered up their belongings, and the boy saw and ran up to join them. He hugged her with his fierce brown arms. "I love you Mom." She didn't answer, but finished packing her beach tote.

Within moments mother and children, without a word to the man, began walking to the parking lot. The man suddenly rose to a sitting position, with the collapsed umbrella next to him, and saw the threesome climbing into the car. When the car started to drive out of the lot without him, he quickly got to his feet. The car disappeared into traffic.

The man had stolen a few grains of sand from the boy's dignity, and the boy had reclaimed it.

Letting Go

She sat there in the car, the bag of his ashes in her lap, long enough for the afternoon to be darkened by eggplant storm clouds pushing inland from the sea. The ocean thrashing the cliffs along the headlands roared like a locomotive.

Julia had managed to avoid this moment for three weeks, since she had received the bizarre phone call. Now it was time to rid herself of the unwanted burden of this packet. She hoped it would give her closure, put an end to the feelings she had locked away for the eight years since she and Paolo had parted.

Slipping her feet out of her pumps, she pulled on sturdy walking shoes over her red tights, then put on a heavy parka and wool gloves. She got out of the car and walked directly into the wind toward a spur of headland that jutted out into the Pacific Ocean. The wind-roiled swells danced with purple and aqua luminescence.

The erratic play of the weather matched her emotions. It had been many years since she'd seen Paolo. The only way she could stop giving in to his attempts to get her back was to put a thousand miles between them. Nothing would ever change. All the facets of Paolo that made him so desirable, were the very things about him that spelled doom for them—his love for life, for his art, for beautiful women, gambling, and the endless lies and pretenses to cover up his excesses. She had finally offered up their love on the altar of reason. Separation physically, if not in heart and mind, was the only way to end their affair.

Then the phone call came. It had taken immense composure to be gracious when Paolo's common-law wife of most of those eight years informed her of his death of cancer.

"I know you once meant a lot to each other," the soft voice over the phone had told her in well-bred, clipped English, with not a hint of unfriendliness.

At first, after Julia moved away, she and Paolo met to give in to their still-insatiable need for each other. In any case it was irrelevant, so long ago. She wondered how the woman knew of her, how to locate her. She must have found Julia's letters. She had warned Paolo after they broke up that he should not keep them, that they would surface one day to hurt someone.

Claire had called to offer her a portion of Paolo's ashes. Julia was mortified, first of all, that this stranger might have read her intimate and graphic letters. More than that, Julia could hardly bear the thought of having a handful of ashes that had once been someone who meant so much to her. She declined on the excuse that Paolo's children and grandchildren should have them.

Then there was Claire's invitation to the memorial service which would take place in two days. Such a bizarre request under the circumstances made her skin prickle with suspicion. Even if she had any intention of going, which she did not, she could not have secured plane reservations at the last minute for a Friday evening flight. If Claire was inviting all of Paolo's previous lovers, Julia had a vision of a church full of beautiful, weeping mystery women swathed in black netting to hide their tears.

Julia used the excuse of the matter of transportation and her work schedule to excuse herself from attending the funeral. As she put the receiver down, she reassured herself she felt no emotion whatsoever at Paolo's passing. They had been lovers, and then friends for a long time. Julia knew of Claire, knew that she and Paolo lived as common-law man and wife, and if Julia met with him on her infrequent trips to see her family still living in her old neighborhood, it was just for a platonic lunch.

So she was stunned when a few days later a package came in the mail containing a copy of Paolo's obituary, which gave great play to his and Claire's glamorous life, and barely mentioning his children and grandchildren. Enclosed was a plastic bag containing a small portion of his ashes.

As Julia followed the trail that threaded across the headlands, the bellowing of the gusts through the sea caves sounded eerie. For an unguarded moment she could imagine Paolo now, from somewhere above, watching the gorse thorns that hemmed in the narrow path clawing at her red tights.

"You look like Santa Claus in those tights," he would have said.

"You do mean the color, I hope," she would have replied.

"Remember how we loved to walk by the ocean?" she felt sure he would have commented. It was the place they felt closest. She'd thought of it often since their separation. That and all the other good memories held her back from looking for love, convincing her she would never again have so intense a connection with anyone.

"I would never have allowed you to wear that. You always looked beautiful for me, and I enjoyed showing you off."

She did remember. When they would pass a man whose eyes swept over her appraisingly, she would feel Paolo draw her arm tighter through his, and nothing more needed to be said.

"Don't talk to me about what was." She shook the bag at the dark sky. "This wasn't my idea, it was Claire's."

"But why are you bringing me here?"

"You're supposed to sprinkle the ashes of the beloved in a place where he has been happy."

"Obviously you couldn't sprinkle them in your

bed."

She could imagine it, his tone teasingly suggestive, his laugh devilish. She scolded herself for remembering him so. He was so much more complicated than his reputation as a Don Juan would suggest.

The wind eased, and the sound of it whistling through the sea caves was like a dirge.

"This was kind of Claire, Paolo, but I have to tell you it's awkward."

"You feel sorry for her, don't you?"

Julia hoped that wherever his presence was reaching to her from, that he had not seen into her thoughts about the funeral scene, all those weeping ex-lovers, all those beautiful eyes underscored with dark half-moons of grief. Paolo loved all women; the difference was measure. His artist's soul required that the ones he loved deeply be unforgettably beautiful.

"Yes, I do feel sorry for Claire. She had the courage to endure all your less lovable attributes."

"We all make our choices, Bella. I never pretended to commit myself wholly to her. Claire and I understood what we needed from each other. We each settled for less than we should have, but in the weighing, that balanced things out and that is why we were together for so long."

"When she called me, I thought at first that you killed yourself, Paolo. At our last lunch together three years ago I felt you were dying of sheer unhappiness. It seemed the life had seeped from you, that you were drained."

She couldn't finish the thought that had crossed her mind then, that he'd regretted the life he'd bargained for with Claire.

Her shoes sank into the rain-soaked earth along the cliffs. In places the path had already given way to the sea and the wind, and the footsteps of determined hikers had begun to beat a new path farther from the edge of the bluffs in the deeper brush.

"Yes, *Cara*, you understood me better than any of the others. But I couldn't have you and I was old enough and tired enough to barter myself for my other needs."

She remembered his words at their last meeting. "I knew in the end you could never accept any less than you gave, Cara. We would've ended badly. You and I each were what we were, so we couldn't ever have been happy together."

"Why are you doing this to me?" she whispered to the deserted headland. She pulled her jacket tight around her. Her hand holding the bag in her pocket felt the rough gravel of his remains.

"Because, *Tesoro*," the wind spoke to her, "I can't leave you until you understand that our choices, yours, mine and Claire's, have never erased what you and I shared. We had to follow our own paths, but you don't have to be afraid of remembering what was real and true. You don't have to be afraid of reaching for that again."

"It's no use bringing this up now, after so long," Julia said to herself—who in reality she was speaking to. Her words and his responses were surely created by her memories and sadness when she learned he had left her for good.

Julia's eyes blurred and for a moment she stumbled and caught herself, horrified to see that her foot was inches from a fissure in the cliff that had eroded the path.

"Are you trying to take me with you?" she thought, filled with a hopeless exasperation with him that she'd experienced too often when they were together.

"The very opposite. I don't think either of us has let ourselves surrender to passion since we parted. My chance is over, but you still have one."

"You're saying you want me to settle, like you did?" She chuckled mirthlessly at her thought.

"No, no, dearest," his words kept reaching to her

from somewhere. Other than the storehouse of her memories? But where? They'd never discussed this.

"I will leave with no regret if I can convince you you still have a chance."

"Then you did will yourself to leave."

"It was the cancer—mostly, but the other, giving up who I was, started long before I became ill."

She suspected that was when the phone calls came from him between his and Claire's forays to Europe and their transatlantic cruises, his voice dull and lifeless. His vitality that seemed to ignite everyone whose life he touched was slowly draining out of him. Finally she had not called him anymore, helpless to ease his despair. He'd brought it on himself. She'd changed her number to an unlisted one.

"I *told* you to destroy my letters after you and Claire were together. I knew they would hurt someone."

"I could not bear to. She had no right to read them after I was gone but even then she wanted to own me completely."

"She loved you very much, Paolo. You were fortunate to find someone to..."

"You realize she called you purposely too late to come to the funeral. She was testing you, hungering to know whether we were lovers all those years when she and I were together. She knew there was someone else in my heart and was obsessed with finding out who it was."

Julia sank down into the seagrass and held her head in her hands. Where was this all coming from? Surely she was fabricating this conversation from everything she'd known, much that she'd guessed, a lot of what she'd held in her memory of the times they'd been together after he'd moved in with Claire.

Was this all being regurgitated by her grief? No, she reminded herself; she wasn't still grieving. He'd been gone to her long before he died.

"I know what you're thinking," he accused.

"You're thinking I was faithful only to Paolo."

"Yes."

"My heart was faithful to you, *Cara*. That is why Claire called you—because she wanted to reassure herself that you no longer had any part of me. When you refused my ashes, that convinced her you didn't."

"I don't think so. I think that is exactly why she sent them, to let me know that she knew." Julia's eyes darted around, looking for a safe outcropping from which she could throw the ashes so that they would not blow back onto the land.

"There," he suggested to her from the susurrating of the waving seagrass, "over by that rock, so that when you walk here you'll see the rock and think of me."

"What, and let you hold on to me for eight more years?"

"I wasn't holding on to you. It is fear of passion that is holding on to you."

Julia was getting tired of these fantastical thoughts whirling around in her head. It was time to end this nonsense. She rushed to the edge of the bluff, parted the zipper opening of the packet and swung it about her in a half circle. She had imagined that the ashes would float out onto the wind in a soft, ethereal cloud, whisking Paolo away to wherever he was destined to travel. Instead, the granular ashes were heavier than she'd thought and they plummeted downward into the surf's spray.

She stood there for a long time, her hand holding the empty bag. The swell rolling through the sea cliffs beneath the headland had calmed and become a velvety moan.

It was time to go. The conversation she'd conjured between them seemed to settle things. She had completed what she'd come to do, so she didn't know what made her turn back for one last look at the place where she'd strewn his ashes, not noticing a rabbit hole

67

just ahead in the center of the path. Her toe caught in it and she found herself flung forcefully to the ground. Dazed by the suddenness of it for a moment, she couldn't get up.

"Need some help?" came the question from nowhere. A fleeting thought that she was still engaged in her imaginary conversation with Paolo made her laugh. But when she looked up a man was standing over her. He was tall and his muscular body was revealed by a tight turtleneck sweater and fitted Levis. She'd not seen him along the cliffs. She had not noticed him around her small town either; she would have remembered.

"Oh, no," she said, embarrassed at her clumsiness. "I can manage." Just then, the wind shifted and the two of them were embraced by an odd warmth. Her mouth dropped in surprise when she saw, dancing on the air, fine sparkling motes of ashes.

She glanced skyward. *Okay, Okay. I get it!*

"I guess I could use a hand up," she admitted. When the hiker pulled her to her feet, instead of meeting the gaze of dark, seductive eyes like Paolo's, she saw that this man had transparent blue eyes that were looking at her with simple friendly interest. His expression was open, and though he was no boy by any means, his smile was boyishly engaging. A smile a woman could trust.

Something odd happened then. The drift of dead ashes and the incessant nattering of the rushing wind dissipated.

She felt like she was walking barefoot beneath a blessedly bright sun on a steamy beach after a long, lonely rain.

Play it as it Lays

More than anything, I wanted to veer out of the "exit only" lane and continue driving. The freeway exit sign I was watching for appeared before I could come up with an honest reason for not exiting.

Though I happened to be in the neighborhood on my way home from a business appointment, I shrank from this visit to my friend. The frightening country of cancer was unfamiliar territory to me. Could I contain my sadness or would I embarrass myself and Lois by being overemotional? I wanted to offer my friend solace, not more distress. What could I say to do that? I had no idea.

I'd brought with me something I hoped would serve to both provide a little entertainment and avoid moments of uncomfortable silence. I resolutely slowed my car and took the freeway exit to continue to the apartment of Lois's brother, where she was staying to be near her doctors and medical resources. Jeremy would be at his office this afternoon.

My hand trembled slightly as I knocked on the door. From inside, a frail but buoyant voice called, "Come in. It's unlocked." I stepped from the glaring afternoon sun into the dim apartment. The heavy curtains were drawn and the air conditioner hummed a cooling mantra. She sat in a rented hospital bed in the center of the living room, surrounded by the paraphernalia of a terminally ill person whose daily furnishings were made up mainly of things that support survival, comfort and distraction.

Her open, easy smile showed little evidence of the grim prognosis of her illness. When my eyes met hers, I was relieved by the calmness in them. I sensed that the religious faith and acceptance that were a part of her stoic New England upbringing had not wavered.

I was barely able to contain my shock at the change in Lois's physical appearance. Scanty tufts of white hair clung to her pink scalp. Her body was ravaged to skeletal dimensions by the illness that was siphoning off her life energy. I willed my gaze away from the mound of the inoperable tumor that pushed out her loose blouse like an unborn child near full term.

We exchanged warm greetings and I set a kitchen chair next to the bed so Lois could bring me up to date on her condition. Knells of unclear diagnoses, more advanced metastasis than suspected and life-threateningly low white cell counts were tempered with her gratitude for the support of family, caring and compassionate doctors and nurses, and correspondence and phone calls from her friends in the town where she lived 120 miles away.

Her manner of describing the series of events, though, was detached, as if she were speaking not of herself, but of a cherished friend who was blessed, considering the circumstances, and for whom a Higher Power had a plan, someone who was taking things a day at a time. It enabled me to level out to an emotionally neutral frame of attention, where I could control the wrench in my midsection.

My initial reluctance to come here was partly due to ignorance. I'd heard a statistic many years before that one in every three people are stricken by cancer. In my large family and among my many friends there had been only one person who had succumbed to cancer, a cousin living on the East Coast. Considering the statistics, I was the blessed exception. As I looked around at my friends whose families were caught up in this terrible illness, I felt lucky to have gotten off so easily.

From time to time I thought of becoming a Hospice volunteer, but I was too frightened of the mystery of death and felt emotionally inadequate to take the hand of someone on the dark journey to that eventuality.

Lois and I, both in our late fifties, had met during my brief stay in her small town near the California coast. Retirement had left me footloose and I needed a quiet time to collect my thoughts and decide in which direction I would go next. I rented half of the duplex she owned at the edge of a Redwood forest.

When we first met, her difficulty walking, a residual of an old spinal injury, kept her nearly housebound. I was a stranger, newly arrived and somewhat shut out by small-town cliquishness.

The magnet of our loneliness drew us into an easy camaraderie, nourished by weekly game nights in her kitchen with tea, home-baked goodies and meaningless chatter about lost loves and far-away grandchildren. Our voices laughing in the night warmed the fortress of our friendship, buffering us from the cold, brooding forest that loomed behind us.

Although we were casual friends brought together by virtue of circumstance, after I relocated to San Francisco, we enjoyed phone calls to each other occasionally. When a number of my voicemails left on her machine weren't returned, I felt uneasy. I'd heard from acquaintances that Lois had no current tenant but attempted to reassure myself that if she'd had an accident her friends who stopped by from time to time would have known.

Weeks later, still having received no response to my calls, I planned a weekend trip to the coast to visit her and put my concern to rest. Before I could do so, she telephoned me. She had been diagnosed with cancer and was staying in the North Bay area to undergo treatment.

I was not close to Lois, but in the scheme of universal consciousness she was a sister making a difficult and painful journey into the unknown. I reassured myself that she had grown children and close friends to look after her, but that didn't relieve me of the feeling that she needed all the support she could get.

But how could I, such a casual friend, be of help? It was that feeling of helplessness, along with my ignorance of her disease, which nearly paralyzed me into inaction.

Our first visit had been lighthearted, full of good expectations. Now I steeled myself as I heard the details of the exploratory surgery that had revealed the tumor to be inoperable. She spoke in an even voice that revealed no fear of the future or any underlying panic at the approach of death. In her narration I heard no plaintive note of forgivable self-pity. I was ashamed to realize that I was selfishly grateful to Lois for not requiring consolation I didn't know how to give.

She described one more chapter in a life whose course and length could be altered from one day to the next by the probing whisk of a surgeon's scalpel or a heartless computer printout of a low white blood count. When she'd brought me up to the present and related her guarded prognosis, she inhaled raggedly, gathering up a sigh that came out not as an exhausted breath of despair, but as a punctuation mark—*there you have it. It is what it is*.

I reached down and opened my tote bag. When she saw I'd brought the Upwords game we'd played when we were neighbors, her face lit up. A spinoff game of Scrabble, it involved a different challenge, constructing connecting words on both a horizontal plane and vertically. She loved learning new words. Her dictionary was within arm's reach whenever we played. Even though I usually won, she never tired of the game.

"I thought if you were feeling well enough we could play."

"I'm a little fuzzy-headed from the treatments. I may be kind of slow," she said, nevertheless reaching out eagerly to help set up the game. It took no more than a few plays for me to become aware that Lois was not playing her usual game consisting of a lot of social chatter and halfheartedly forming words on a level plane constructing short, commonplace interlinking words.

This afternoon her customary compliments about the words I built smacked more of a diversionary tactic. She would cleverly spot opportunities to build words vertically and change as many as three interconnected words by the placement of two or three letter tiles. She was unstoppable, determined to win. Because she was suffering so much loss in her life at this point, I truly wanted her to trounce me, even if it meant my choosing some easy moves that didn't garner me many points.

I didn't have to. The game proceeded at a surprisingly brisk pace, slowed only by sips of herbal tea and forkfuls of the moist marble cake I had baked and brought, remembering it was Lois's favorite dessert. So focused were we, that her bed, the game board and my chair seemed like planets illuminated by the sun of the goose-necked lamp over the bed, drifting in the dark galaxy of the room, far from hospitals and clinics where one hoped the poison pumped into one's body would kill the disease before it killed one's body.

The score was nearly tied when we reached the point at which each of us was left with one letter tile. I scanned the board to see where I could use my last tile, the letter "i," to change an existing word.

At the center of the board, the word "due" leapt out at me. *Aha*, I thought, reaching for my tile to place the "i" over the "u." I stopped my hand in midair, mortified. I would rather lose the game than alter the word to read "die."

I searched the game board for another way to use my "i" tile as frantically as one would search for an exit after a fire alarm has gone off. I could pretend ignorance and simply take a five-point penalty for not using my last tile, but I knew once the game was over and my tile was turned up, Lois, in her usual helpful way, would scan the board to suggest where I might have put that tile to beat her, and would find me out.

There had to be another place to use the "i" tile. The air conditioner seemed to thrum impatiently. Finally I spotted a letter "n" I could place the "i" in front of. Relieved, I changed the word to "in" and tallied my score.

"We're tied, Lois," I taunted, animated by my relief. "Give it your best shot."

Without a moment's hesitation, Lois took her last tile and smacked it right down on the word "due," covering the letter "u." She moved her hand away, revealing that her last tile had also been the letter "i."

"I won!" she sang.

My eyes were momentarily riveted on the word. I pulled myself together quickly and put my hands on my hips in mock exasperation.

"Fuzzy-headed? You set me up!"

Her self-satisfied expression was sweetly pardonable. I managed to avert my eyes by making a fuss of checking my watch.

"Oh, I lost track of time! I want to get home ahead of the rush hour."

Lois's polite but weak smile didn't cover her disappointment. "Already?"

We'll play again soon, but look out next time," I cautioned.

"I'm glad you stopped by--" She paused, thoughtfully as if weighing whether to go on. "Not many people visit me anymore."

I wanted to ease her sadness. Before I'd come, I'd dreamed up a great big bagful of excuses to ease my conscience in an attempt to avoid this sad visit. They hadn't worked for me and I didn't think they would justify her friends' abandonment of her.

We'd always been somewhat restrained with each other, but when she held her hand out to shake mine, I couldn't help but carefully put my arms around her fragile body and hold her momentarily. I wasn't going to say "good-bye." Not yet. I put the Upwards game into my tote bag and said, without considering how long it took to drive directly here, "I want a rematch. I'll see you in a few days."

Her face brightened with anticipation, smoothing out its harsh lines of pain.

As I stepped into the brilliant tangerine glow of the early evening and turned to pull the door closed, I saw Lois waving feebly from her cocoon of light, suspended in the dark certainty of her future. The purpose of my visit had been to give comfort to Lois. It was she, however, who provided it to me.

The Best Tomato

I was going around the corner in the main corridor of my mother's residential care facility when I nearly ran into a resident coming my way.

Despite my determination to not be rude and stare, I couldn't take my eyes off her. Her enormously wide-brimmed straw hat, heaped with faded silk flowers of many varieties, jiggled pompously as she tottered along in tired high heels that had been fashionable forty years ago. I admired women who had the courage to hang on forever to certain clothing or jewelry they loved despite the changing fashion trends. She'd hung on through quite a number of changes.

Her Cindy Crawford red lipstick had bled into the puckered lines around her mouth. Beneath a shoulder slightly stooped by osteoporosis, she clasped a patent leather clutch bag of an outdated style one might find at the bottom of a thrift store bin.

In this lackluster place where life seemed to have run out of gas, the woman's brilliant plumage was a fresh breath of air. Residents in wheelchairs and walkers, forewarned of her approach by the sound of her high heels rapping along the linoleum floor, parted like the Red Sea.

As we continued, both walking towards the foyer, she seemed to glide along on an electrical current, the air fairly crackling with her energy.

"Good morning," I said. "What a wonderful hat!"

"Thank you, dear. I'm on my way to the market. They have the *best* tomatoes." A small net bag of the type my grandmother had to carry her purchases home from the green grocer's was slung over her arm. I was curious as to why she was shopping for groceries when

77

the assisted care home cooked all meals and served them to residents in the community dining room.

From my observations, most of the residents were confined to beds or wheelchairs, their immobility which protected them from straying from the home. When I saw her make a dash for the exit, I was concerned for her safety. After she breezed ahead of me out the door, I expected an alarm to be triggered by a security bracelet of the type my mother wore. When there was only silence in her wake, I concluded the staff must feel she could manage on her own.

As I walked to my car, I saw her approach a gardener who was edging a lawn nearby. She said a few words and he put down his gardening tool and held out his arm to her as gallantly as an escort at a cotillion. She took it and the young man led her across the busy street. I couldn't remember the last time a man had offered me his arm to cross a street. This little lady could probably teach me a few things.

I drove to my daughter's home two blocks away to pick up a list of errands she'd asked me to do for her while she was at work. I was helping myself to a glass of water in the kitchen, when I looked out the window and spotted a familiar cluster of faded silk flowers seeming to bob along the top of the garden hedge on its own volition until, at the end of the row of hedges, Amelia seemed suddenly to reconnect to her hat and stopped to bend and pet a waiting cat that rubbed familiarly against her thin, bluish legs.

The telephone rang; it was my daughter calling to make sure I'd found the shopping list she'd left on the kitchen table.

"By the way," I commented, "there's an interesting lady from Grandma's residential care home walking down the street. She's wearing a big hat with flowers —"

"Amelia," my daughter said. "She's taking her daily walk to the market."

"She'll be all right?"

"Oh, yes. Everyone in the neighborhood knows her. She's very cautious about traffic and such, so they let her leave the home."

Let her leave, I thought. It sounded like a prisoner being let out on furlough. But that was the very reason my mother had been moved to the home, to protect her from her confused and unsafe nocturnal wanderings away from her former apartment. She was protected her, but confined, nonetheless.

I was getting into my car, the list of errands in hand, when I heard the cooing of baby talk a short distance up the block. An elderly man walking a small, leashed terrier had stopped to talk to Amelia, who was searching for something in her net bag. As I drove away, I could see the little dog sitting back on the scruffy tripod of its rigid little tail and hind legs, begging with a pretty tilt of its head for the anticipated treat in Amelia's outstretched hand. I felt a wave of regret that my mother no longer showed an interest in anyone but her closest family members.

The last errand on my list was to stop at the market for groceries, and magazines for my mother. When I rolled my cart into the produce section, there was Amelia in front of the tomato display looking over the newly stocked salad and Roma tomatoes with a careful eye. She gingerly held a few of them, making a fuss over choosing one.

As I wheeled my cart about, bagging my produce as I went, I became aware that whenever a shopper approached to select some tomatoes, Amelia would strike up a conversation with her.

I heard the words "tomato pie," and saw that Amelia and a young woman had their heads close together, the old one reciting as the young one jotted down ingredients on the back of a grocery list. As I looked through the lettuce heads nearby for a firm iceberg, a produce man who was putting out fresh bananas paused to compliment Amelia on her final choice of a tomato, plump and smooth, with not a bruise on it.

"You sure do know your tomatoes, Mrs. Hill," he said. Amelia bestowed a demure smile on him.

When I got to the checkout stand, I caught a glimpse of straw and faux blossoms at the next register. Amelia was giving the bagger instructions.

"First wrap it in one of those soft plastic bags, dear, so it won't get bruised, and then put that in a paper bag so it will stay nice and cool."

"Yes, Ma'am," the girl answered in a monotone, making a show of wrapping the purchase under Amelia's watchful eye. I always do it just the way you say."

I dropped my daughter's grocery items at her home and drove back to the retirement home to bring my mother her magazines.

On the way to her room I saw Amelia's name on a nameplate on the door of a room. The door was ajar and I leaned in to say *hello*. Only the maid was there, cleaning the room. On a small chest of drawers in front of the window sat four tomatoes. Two had ripened in the sun and fruit flies were sitting on them. Unaware of my presence at the door, the maid furtively swept them all into a trash bag in her hand. When she turned and saw me, she jumped back, startled.

Her expression of guilt fled and she smiled at me. "I'm sorry, I thought you were Amelia."

"I just wanted to say hello to her." I nodded toward the bag. "She must love tomatoes."

"She doesn't eat them at all." That's why we have to throw them out—when she's not here or she would get upset.

I delivered the magazines to my mother and was on my way out to my car when Amelia came into the foyer and passed me.

"Good morning, Amelia."

80

She hesitated a moment, studying me uncertainly, but apparently decided from my familiar greeting that we must know each other because her face relaxed into a smile.

Before I could remind her we'd met earlier, she leaned over confidentially, as if she were about to share some juicy morsel of gossip with me, and laid her hand on my arm.

"Would you like to see my tomato? I've been to the market and they have the *best* tomatoes."

"You don't say," I said, charmed by her enthusiasm.

I admired the tomato she took from the net bag to show me. It was perfectly shaped, at the peak of its ripeness, and smelled like warm dusty sunshine.

"Did you know, dear, that a tomato is not a vegetable at all? It's a fruit—a citrus fruit." Then she whispered, "The French believed tomatoes could arouse passion. They called them 'love apples'."

"Imagine that," I answered. "I think I'll have to serve them to my husband more often."

I gave her a small wave and walked on. I thought about Amelia's quest for the best tomato and wondered if she realized what a marvelous gift she'd given me that day, reminding me that life, like her tomato, is what we make of it.

The Rag Doll

Her sister led her up the squeaky wooden stairs of her new mother-in-law's house. As they passed the window on the landing, Lulu saw that the black piney woods were full of fireflies. The sight of them always made her heart sing, but tonight it only reminded her of the last time she and Samuel had lain in each other's arms beneath the thick old trees, watching the fireflies dance among the witch's hand branches. Something that could never happen again.

Sara led her to the bed and avoided Lulu's eyes as she slipped the scratchy new night dress, a wedding gift from J.J.'s ma, over her thin body.

"There, Lulee, that should stop you from shaking so."

Lulu clenched her teeth together to keep them from chattering. The ebb and flow of conversation at the wedding dinner downstairs rose through the thin floorboards. Sara pulled her hairbrush through Lulu's kinky red curls, a lot more gently than usual.

"You'll be better off here," her sister said softly. Lulu knew that was true. It would mean an end to the strappings she got from Pa during his liquor-fed despair. Beatings so bad she had scars on her legs from where the buckle had cut her.

"It breaks my heart to see you hungry when it's a bad year on the farm. You'll always have plenty to eat now."

Lulu doubted *that.* The odor of Mother Farley's badly dressed pork roast with too many onions had seeped beneath the bedroom door. Her stomach squeezed. It smelled just like the raw stink of their hog pens.

83

She saw the tears glistening in Sara's eyes in the sickly yellow lamplight as she bent to help her get beneath the covers.

Sara kissed her cheek. "Now, you leave that light on for your husband. You be a good girl and do as he says." Her voice softened when she added, "You'll get used to it." When she turned to go, she paused at the door as if she had forgotten something she wanted to tell Lulu, but then went out and quietly closed the door.

Lulu thought *be a good girl*. She wasn't a girl anymore, she guessed. She'd started her monthlies last summer, right after her 13th birthday.

J.J. had always seemed like an old uncle. Now Lulu realized when Sara had asked her if she liked him, she should not have been polite and answered that she liked him fine. She should have told her sister that he sometimes looked at her with hungry eyes like the old fox that Lulu'd surprised lurking near the duck pond.

Lots of times J.J. pretended to accidentally brush his hand on her hip or breast when she walked by him. Nothing real bad, just kinda sneaky. When that had happened with Samuel it was wonderful. When J.J. did it, it made her want to wash herself.

She pushed aside the covers and padded across the room to the dresser to the flour sack that held her few belongings. In the darkness she felt for the familiar softness of Junie. Back in bed, Lulu held Junie against her and tried to picture her mother who died giving birth to her. All she had to go by was her parents' old wedding picture in Sara's room. That was all that was left of her now. That, and Junie, the love-worn rag doll that her mother had made when she was carrying Lulu in her belly.

The talking downstairs droned on. Mother Farley had forbade a shivaree and said a family dinner was more pleasing to the Lord. When Lulu's friend Patsy had married her Henry, it was different. Patsy was very old, almost 18, and Henry just a year older. They were

like two moony-eyed possums. They just belonged
together, plain as day. She remembered how jealous she
felt at their shivaree, what with all the drinkin' and
dancin', but mostly of the way Patsy's eyes were shining
when her friends led her upstairs to get her ready for
her new husband.

Now she listened for the dreaded sound of
scraping chairs that would signal the end of the dinner.
She wished she could hear her stepbrother's voice, but
she guessed he wasn't saying much tonight. Early that
morning she had gone to gather the eggs from Sara's
scrawny hens, fussing over them because it would be the
last time she would do so. As she talked to them she
began to cry. Samuel stepped out from behind the
henhouse and startled her.

"I'm gonna miss you, Lulee," he had told her
quietly, reaching out to gently wipe away her tears with
his forefinger. She knew how he felt. Her marriage to
J.J. would build an invisible wall between them. His
sunny smile that always brought a playful sparkle to his
eyes didn't appear to help lift her heart. There was
nothing to smile about.

"Now that we'll be kin, I'll be able to call you
Brother and mean it," Lulu had said to cheer him. His
expression told her she'd failed miserably.

"I could *never* be your *brother*," he spat, and
then swiped his eyes with his forearm.

Samuel was only two years older than she, but
fifteen years younger than J.J. The men were as
different as could be because they had different pa's.

Footsteps on the stairway broke into her
thoughts. She held her breath for a moment, and then
let out a sigh of relief. They were light footsteps. Oh, if it
were only Samuel! It was impossible, but
maybe...maybe...The door opened, and her heart
dropped like a heavy stone.

The stick of a woman walked to the bed, seeming
to grow menacingly as she came towards the lamp and

its garish light cast her ballooning shadow on the wall behind her.

"I come to say I welcome you into this God-fearing family, Daughter. You be an obedient Christian wife to my son and you'll have a good life here. Surely better'n what you had." Her face looked like a dried apple when she frowned and demanded none too softly, "You hear me, girl?"

"Yes, Ma'am," Lulu could barely whisper.

"In the mornin' Brother will show you how to make breakfast. Then you'll help weed out the old hens and butcher them."

Lulu shuddered. She had never gotten used to Sara's poor chickens scrambling away from the chopping block without their heads, running around for a few minutes while the last few desperate pumps of their hearts fooled their legs into thinking everything was okay.

She nodded obediently. Her new mother-in-law left the room. Lulu realized that even though she and Samuel would now be brother and sister, living here in the same house would ease her.

She thought of the days they had crossed the fallen logs over the river, or lain in the new hay and rolled together, laughing as they tickled each other playfully, or elbow to elbow stargazing on a blanket with their toes touching in the summer woods. The yearning that swelled her heart and flooded the secret places of her body was like a shaming finger shaking a warning at her.

A scrape of chairs pushing across the dining room floor brought her up sharp. The conversation had stopped. The sudden quiet made the hair on her arms prickle. The footsteps on the stairs were heavy this time, bearing the considerable weight of her new husband.

By the time he opened the door, Lulu had willed herself into limp acceptance. She would obey. She would do it for Sara who knew best and only wanted to help her. Samuel would never know she had once hoped in her heart the footsteps on the stairs would be his.

The door creaked open slowly and J.J. closed it quietly behind him. His expression seemed strange to her, one of awkwardness, yet his eyes turned toward the bed and burned into her. She watched him, with the blanket drawn up to her chin. He came to stand over her and pulled the quilt away, revealing Junie in Lulu's arms.

When he reached for the doll, her hands clenched around it. She couldn't stop the sob that exploded from some struggling place deep down inside her. If she let go of her Junie there would be nothing between them.

He firmly took it from her. "You're Lucinda Mae Farley now, not a young'un anymore. You can keep this for our babies." He tossed Junie across the room. The doll hit the clouded dresser mirror and slid down into a jumbled lump. Without taking his eyes off Lulu, J.J. pulled the suspenders off his shoulders and lowered his pants.

When J.J. was done with her, Lulu felt like Junie, a jumbled lump. She closed her eyes and wondered if, like Sara's headless hens, she would run around for a while thinking everything was all right before she realized she was dead.

Wheeling through Life

I disagree that a passion for cars is the exclusive right of the male; I've loved the cars I've owned. Granted, I wasn't as interested in what was beneath the hood as I was with the look of a car, how it made me feel, and where it could take me.

At 15 1/2 years of age, I obtained a learner's permit. My dad gave me combat driving lessons. Before I could apply for my license, however, I had to complete High School Driver Education. After my first class, my instructor shakily pointed to the St. Christopher medal pinned to the sun visor in the training car and suggested I get one of my very own.

"My dad taught me to drive. He was a taxi cab driver in Chicago."

"Ahhh, *that* explains it."

After my instructor sweated through five sessions of what he diplomatically referred to as "fine-tuning" my driving skills, I got my license.

To earn money for my first car, I got a job clerking at a roadside fruit stand. By the age of 17, I had saved up enough money for a down payment on my first car. My dad and I made the rounds of used car lots. When I laid eyes on the 1956 Dodge with its sleek streamlined look and jet fins, I fell in love for the first time in my life—and it was not with a boy. Faded paint and dulled chrome couldn't diminish the elegant look of it. The interior was cool mock white leather, the radio speakers rocked the car with no static at full volume, and the car featured a push button transmission.

Dad spent twenty minutes under the hood and crawled out to say the engine was in good shape. The bank wouldn't give me a loan because of my age, so Dad lent me the money—at the same interest rate the bank charged.

I was transformed. My blemishes cleared up and I became instantly popular. The balloon payment owing to my dad required disciplined management of my meager fruit stand earnings. I would fill only two gallons of gas at a time to monitor my fuel budget. After Dad came to my rescue with a gas can a few times he made me join an automobile club road service. I didn't know anything about changing spark plugs, but I knew how to wax a car, polish chrome, and keep the white interior dazzling.

Within a couple months I cockily presented him with the balloon payment in snappy new $100 bills. It was the final payment on my emancipation. I saved up again to have the car painted creamy white and satin forest green, after which for some unknown reason it seemed to go a lot faster. A traffic cop pulled me over for going 89 miles per hour on a deserted country road— deserted except for him hiding behind a huge bush. His eyes flicked admiringly over my car. He gave me a stern lecture and a warning, and let me go. He understood.

I have pleasant memories of the cars I've owned that were equipped with an endless array of features: stick shift, push-button shift, and automatic shift; wide whitewalls, deluxe wood-grained dashboards, and imported stereo systems; hard-tops, hatchbacks, sunroofs and moon roofs; delicious paints like candy apple red, shimmering forest green, and flecked gold. I managed this on my modest earnings by buying at end-of-the-model-year discounts, or showroom demo cars and lease vehicles that didn't have a lot of miles on them.

After my children moved out to live on their own, for the first time in my life I could finally afford to shop for a new car with all the equipment and add-on's I wanted.

In March, a salesman at a local dealership took a hefty deposit from me, and, with my list of non-negotiables in hand, he assured me he would locate the car I was looking for.

Three months later he got back to me with an inventory of the unsold models for that year, none of them having the bells and whistles I had specified. He knew he had a hysterical woman on his hands, so he promised to get me one of the last cars coming off the assembly line in Detroit, equipped exactly the way I wanted it, if I would be willing to wait until the end of August.

At the end of August I learned that the assembly line for that year's model had shut down before my car could be assembled. To vent my frustration, and not really expecting any response, I wrote a letter to the president of the General Motors. To my surprise, he (or most likely his admin assistant's admin assistant) replied with a letter of apology, promising me at the start of production I would get the coming year's model for the price of the previous year's model.

In October the dealership had my car, hot off the line, equipped as I had specified. Driving home in a delirium of joy, I went two miles out of my way following a milk truck so I could admire myself in my new car reflected in the back of the aluminum trailer.

On a clear day the sunroof would be left behind in the garage, and I would drive up the coast, the sun warming the age lines from my face, the wind whipping the gray from my hair. I wrote a thank you note to the president of the company, telling him that the delivery of that car had taken nearly as long as my first pregnancy but it was worth every minute of the wait.

Because I traveled a lot for my work, my car and I shared endless hours on the road. I felt as nostalgic about it as the Beach Boys when they sang, "In my Room," only I found refuge in my car, insulated from all the woes of the world.

My car was my big toy that hauled around all my little toys. Where earlier models had transported infant seats, playpens and girl scouts, this one hauled paints and easel, sailboat parts, cameras and tripods, scuba gear, a crab trap, skis, and a boogie board.

It carried armloads of wildflowers, Christmas trees whose dropped pine needles blessed the car with their fragrance for weeks, and trunk loads of beach driftwood for the fireplace. There was adventure too, back roads that beckoned, hard-packed beaches to race down at sunset, and blinding snowstorms and sandstorms to sweat through together.

Time passed, but my car always seemed new and racy to me. The first sign that it was getting on in years was when pieces of molded plastic seat parts would mysteriously appear on the floorboard. Next, the seat belts became frayed.

My tape player developed an appetite for my favorite cassettes and dined on them regularly. One of my speakers would short out for no reason. Quite by chance I discovered if I ran over the speed bump in my condominium complex parking lot at a certain angle and speed, the wiring would make contact again and the speaker would resume playing. I knew that car so well, I could tell by the sound of the engine when it needed oil.

The directional turning signal arm on which the windshield wiper switch was located broke. To hold the arm in place to be sure the turn signal would continue to function, I administered some first aid with electrical tape, which worked fine and matched the black interior.

What I didn't realize was my patchwork interfered with the functioning of the wipers. The next time it rained I was able to turn them on, but not off. A helpful neighbor removed the wiper's fuse from beneath the dashboard to stop the wipers. He put it in his pocket so it wouldn't get mislaid and forgot to give it to me.

On my way to work the next morning it began to rain. I pulled over to the side of the road. With my owner's manual in one hand, curled up in a fetal position with my head under the dashboard, I rooted around in the fuse panel for a fuse with the same amperage that I could borrow to use in the wiper fuse slot. I found one for the interior lights, removed it, and put it on the seat next to me.

As I drove, it would rain intermittently, which meant that I would have to keep one hand on the wheel and use the other to alternately insert and remove the fuse when it started and stopped raining by feeling for the correct slot in the fuse box beneath the dash. And kids today think computer games take a lot of dexterity!

My innovative temporary solutions could not avoid the inevitable. A gas station attendant, while checking my water, told me it sounded like I had a hole in the manifold valve, but the cost of repair was way down on the list of my budget priorities. I soothed my worry by convincing myself the rapping noise sounded rather racy. One day the hatchback shade rolled up on its very own with a lusty snap, never to unroll again.

After nine years, the 120,000-plus miles on the odometer were beginning to concern me. I had the car painted, hoping to make me—and perhaps it— feel a little more hopeful, like Botox for a used car. It was a cheap paint job, all I could afford at the time. The color was flecked gold, and what it lacked in quality, it made up in sparkle.

The undercarriage of the automobile began to make a frighteningly loud noise. I got an estimate of $1500 at the local body shop to weld some structural damage. The welder said I was probably hitting parking lot speed bumps too hard. Next time the radio speaker stopped working, it stayed that way.

I have to say that as timeworn as it became, that car never lost its appeal for me. Like a spouse who looks at her man each day and sees not the receding hairline, nor the widening waistline, but the male essence of the young stud she fell in love with, I still saw my car as that snazzy hardtop convertible reflected in the milk truck trailer so many years ago.

The sad day I was at the bank applying for a loan so I could trade my car in for a new one, a young janitor who was cleaning up looked out the window and spotted the "For Sale" sign in my car window. His eyes glazed over with longing and I knew I had a taker.

Because of the repairs needed, I was asking a bargain price. But I could see he wasn't in a frame of mind to think rationally, so to be fair, I insisted he take it to a mechanic so he'd know what he was getting into. The next day he picked up the car and peeled off some of what little rubber was left on the tires as he sped off to his mechanic.

When he brought the car back to me, he recited all the repairs needed and the cost. As he droned on, I was mentally subtracting the cost of each repair from the asking price, quickly coming to the conclusion that I might have to pay him to take the car off my hands.

He finished reading his list and stunned me when he promptly handed me my asking price in cash. He had the same "have-to-have-it" look on his face I had when I saw my first car on the used car lot.

The buyer jumped in and revved the engine. The rapping of the leaky manifold reverberated throughout the parking lot and he grinned with satisfaction. He drove off with the windshield wipers thumping away on a dry windshield.

He hit a speed bump in the parking a lot faster than he should have. The undercarriage clanged loudly and the stereo suddenly blasted out "In My Room," the audiotape it had digested two months before and had refused to regurgitate.

As the car rounded a curve and disappeared from sight, I stood at the curb, left with a small handful of cash and a big head full of happy memories. I couldn't help it; tears welled in my eyes as I watched that old car drive off to new adventures without me.

www.ingramcontent.com/pod-product-compliance
Lightning Source LLC
Chambersburg PA
CBHW052033260626
47163CB00006B/297